Muggleton

Kalangadoo
Letter from

Political satirist, writer, performer and photographer Bryan Dawe has enjoyed a long career on radio, television, film and the speakers' circuit with his characters Sir Murray Rivers QC and Roly Parks.

Bryan has worked for 26 years with fellow satirist John Clarke in one of the longest running national segments on Australian television, *Clarke & Dawe*, aired every Thursday night on the ABC. He was a cast member of the highly acclaimed ABC television series *The Games* and has appeared in various films, including the hit Australian film *The Castle*.

Among his photographic exhibitions, Bryan contributed to a joint exhibition in 2014 called *Syria Lost*, documenting his various journeys to Syria before the civil war.

Bryan is an inveterate traveller with a particular penchant for long train journeys in foreign places.

Letter from Kalangadoo
The Roly Parks Collection

BRYAN DAWE

UWA PUBLISHING

First published in 2015 by
UWA Publishing
Crawley, Western Australia 6009
www.uwap.uwa.edu.au

UWAP is an imprint of UWA Publishing,
a division of The University of Western Australia.

THE UNIVERSITY OF
WESTERN AUSTRALIA
Achieve International Excellence

National Library of Australia Cataloguing-in-Publication entry:
Dawe, Bryan, author.
Letter from Kalangadoo / Bryan Dawe.
ISBN: 9781742587639 (paperback)
Australian wit and humour.
Kalangadoo (S.A.)—Fiction.
A823.4

Typeset in Bembo by Lasertype
Printed by McPhersons Printing Group

For
Jody Seidel (Sonya Parks)
who was there at the very beginning

CONTENTS

You – you alone will have the stars as no one else has them...In one of the stars I shall be living. In one of them I shall be laughing. And so it will be as if all the stars were laughing, when you look at the sky at night...You – only you – will have stars that can laugh.

Antoine de Saint-Exupéry, The Little Prince

CYRIL & THE MARRIAGE
COUNSELLOR

Kalangadoo, Monday

Dear Gene,

How are you son?

Sorry I haven't written for a while but with one thing or another, I've been so busy for the last few weeks I haven't had time to scratch myself. On top of everything else Cyril died last Monday and your sister and I spent most of the week trying to cheer your mother up.

She's taken it pretty hard of course. After all, Cyril has been with her for – I don't know how many years it is now, it's got to be ten. It's very sad, but he had a good life.

We ended up burying him down the backyard next to the shed alongside Fang the cat and Harold the parrot. Thought Cyril would like that, you know, at least he'd have some company.

I take it you knew old Fang passed away, I'm sure your mum would have written and told you. Funny how it happened too. He was sitting there one minute staring at Cyril in the budgie cage, the next minute he was as dead as a doornail. Just like that. Not a bad way to go I suppose – it's better than getting run over by a truck, isn't it? Wouldn't mind going that way myself, come to think of it. Staring up at the budgie one minute, on your way to heaven the next.

So how have you been getting along, Gene? Hope you're winning.

I'm doing all right, I was a bit lousy for a while there after your mum and I parted ways, but I'm starting to kick with the wind again now.

My back is playing up a bit, my left knee is still crook and my liver is a bit dodgy according to Doctor Wilson, but aside from that I can't complain. Not much point is there? I mean there's no one around to complain to.

Your mother and I are talking to each other, that's the main thing. I suppose it would be a bit hard not to talk to each other after 54 years. I don't think my good ear would know what to do with itself if it didn't hear your mum's voice in it once a day. You've got to laugh, don't you?

Your sister Sharon has been beaut too, she comes around every couple of days to say hello and make sure I'm eating properly. She keeps bringing me around this macrobiotic food she eats and those bloody lentil things. Gene, that stuff would kill you if you ate it for too long. I tell her I eat it but, just between you and me, I wait until she's gone and I sling it over the fence to the Davisons' chooks. But don't tell Sharon that though, will you? She means well.

Anyway your mum and I are still going to the marriage counsellor. I don't know what she's told you. I'm a bit jack of it all to tell you the truth and it's starting to give me the willies.

I didn't know I had so many things wrong with me, Gene. I tell you what, once your mum gets into gear at these little get-togethers, there's no stopping her. I had to start writing all the complaints down, I couldn't keep up with her. I'm not saying she hasn't got a case, but dearie me, your mum's going on about stuff that happened 40 years ago.

I said to her, 'Sonya, I can't remember what happened yesterday let alone how I put your nose out of joint at a bloody barbecue at Alf's place in 1953. I mean, fair crack of the whip! If it was getting on your quince, why did you leave it for 40 years to have a shot at me?'

'I only just realised it annoyed me,' she said.

I don't know Gene, it's got me beat. She's a mystery, your mother.

Oh, did your mum tell you that Sharon's husband, Geoff, got a promotion down there at the Department of Births, Deaths & Marriages? He's been made Senior Certificate Officer or something like that in the birth certificate section. He's as happy as Larry. He gets a free trip to Adelaide once a year and reckons if he does all right in this, he might have a shot at archives. Good on him.

Anyway Gene, I better saddle up and get cracking, I've got to have a go at cooking myself a bit of spaghetti for tea and there's a bit of a wingding on next door at the Davisons for Ted's birthday. They invited me to join them and I thought I might toddle over a bit later. I'll let you know how the spaghetti turns out anyway.

Give my regards to 'Robert Helpmann'. I hope the ballet business is working out for him. Write soon.

Lots of love,
Your dad

THE ANZAC DAY MARCH

Kalangadoo, Monday

Dear Gene,

How are you son?

Well, I'm recovering. My leg's a bit better and I'm moving about the place now in a wheelchair. You've got to keep moving at my age, Gene, keep the parts moving; you stop and you can't get the body going again. I've seen jokers at my age go downhill really quickly in this condition.

Anyway, what have I been up to? Not a lot really. I had an outing on Monday – my mate Milton was marching on Anzac Day in Mount Gambier so Percy Struthers and Milton piled me and the wheelchair into the car and I went down to watch them march. Well, I was going to just watch, but what happened was this old codger in another wheelchair saw me in the crowd and came up and had a go at me because I wasn't in the march.

Cantankerous old bugger he was, well he seemed like it at the time anyway. Talk about giving a joker a hard time.

'What's the matter with you, digger?' he demanded. 'You don't look dead, why aren't you marching?'

I explained the situation to him, I mean you know the story, Gene: your mum and I didn't fight in the war, we sang, we entertained the troops. So I tell him this and told him they wouldn't let us march, because you had to have been a soldier to march. 'Says who?' demanded the old codger.

'Well, whoever says who,' I said.

He just looked at me Gene and said, 'Bugger the ones who "says who" mate, we took notice of "says who's" in France in 1916 and look where that got us!'

Anyway, I could see he wasn't going to let up so I wheeled myself into line and ended up marching instead of watching for the first time in 40 years.

Turns out to be a beaut old fellow too, Morrie – Morrie Parsons his name is. Reckons he was at the business end of 90, but only looks a day over 80 and is as tough as nails. Morrie still lives on his own, he's a bloody marvel and a funny bugger too. He said to me, 'I'm glad you came along Roly, I've been thinking it's about time we had a recruitment drive. I'm the last one left you know. The rest of the buggers died on me, haven't they?'

Well, the upshot of it all is that Morrie's made me an honorary member of his regiment. He's talked me into marching again with him next year. If for some reason he doesn't front up, he made me promise I'd march in the regiment anyway. I promised that I would, I couldn't let the side down could I?

Anyway, I better go. One of the tyres on my wheelchair has gone down and I've got to go and find a pump from somewhere.

Regards to Ahmed. Write soon.

Lots of love,
Your dad

OLD DOC WILSON &
THUNDERBOXES

Kalangadoo, Monday

Dear Gene,

How are you son? You winning?

I'm all right myself. The liver is playing up a bit, the back is a bit crook and my bad knee is no better. Oh, the cholesterol and blood sugar levels are up a bit and the new heart tablets are giving me wind, but aside from that, I'm a picture of health really.

As old Doc Wilson said to me, 'At least it takes your mind off the arthritis, Mr Parks.'

He has an exceptional bedside manner, Doc Wilson. Milton Jones reckons Doc Wilson's lost his marbles. I think he's right. I reckon he's in the book, he just doesn't know what page he's on.

I said to Doc Wilson a few weeks ago after my knee was still playing up, 'Look, Doctor, maybe I should get a second opinion?' Doc Wilson looked at me and said, 'All right, if you insist. Come back tomorrow at 2 pm.'

He's really losing it Gene, he shouldn't be practising.

Milton had an appointment to get something shoved up his Khyber the other day and, while sitting in the waiting room, out from the doctor's surgery comes old Bluey Jackson so Milton asked him how he was. Bluey replied, 'Oh, Doc Wilson reckons I'm as fit as a mallee bull.'

Then what do you know, Gene, the words had no sooner come out of his mouth when Bluey drops dead in Doc Wilson's doorway. Milton said the nurse ran up, checked his pulse and yelled out: 'Doctor Wilson! Doctor Wilson! The man is dead! What do we do?'

Doc Wilson looks at the nurse and says, 'Turn him around and make it look as if he's arriving.'

He needs to be put out to pasture, Doc Wilson. You take your life into your own hands when you turn up to his clinic.

Speaking of people trying to get rid of us oldies, the government here is in on it too. They want us dead so they don't have to pay us the pension. The young are also in on the scheme; they want us dead so they can get their hands on our assets quicker. They are trying to confuse us to death Gene, how else do you explain a DVD remote? Who the hell came up with that device? It's the most confusing thing ever invented.

I bought one of these home entertainment centres or whatever they're called a few weeks ago. I knew I couldn't put the bloody thing together and Sharon was away, so Milton and three of my other mates come round to my place one night to try and help me figure it out.

Five blokes over 75, with 375 years of experience among us – do you reckon we could get that bugger to work? Bloody thing!

In the end I rang my neighbour who sent his ten-year-old grandson around the next day to set it up for me – which he did in under five minutes.

The whole corporate sector is doing it as well; if they're not selling you products that you can't operate when you get home, they're flogging you phone or electricity deals a barrister would be flat out trying to make sense of. If, by some miracle, you can work it all out, the bloody font size is so tiny you can't possibly read the fine print.

Confuse us to death, that's what everyone is trying to do Gene. I mean, I know a few of the oldies down our way who still haven't figured out how a stereo works. In fact, one or two of them down here are still coming to grips with inside toilets that flush.

I can still remember when they first converted the old thunderboxes to inside toilets. There were some people down this way who tried to bring their thunderboxes inside. I know, I was one of them.

As old Bern Colville, Hazel Colville's husband – he's dead now Bern, of course – said to me at the time: 'They're a bloody marvel these indoor lavatories, Roly.'

I said, 'They are.'

'Yeah,' he said. 'How you can push a button and it all ends up over at Bluey Dodson's night cart – that's a bloody miracle.'

'It is.'

'I'll tell you one thing about them, though,' said Bern. 'They don't like sawdust much, do they?'

Give my regards to Ahmed, won't you? Write soon.

Lots of love,
Your dad

9

RAINING PEA SOUP

Kalangadoo, Monday

Dear Gene,

How are you son? Keeping the dingoes off the front step?

I hope so. I've been a bit up and down myself, to tell you the truth. You know how you have those miserable weeks when, truly, if it was raining pea soup, you'd get hit on the head by a fork – thrown by your mother!

I'm telling you, I couldn't take a trick in that department this week. Couldn't look at your mum without getting my head bitten off!

She'd been a bit crook, as you know, so I tried to do the right thing: keep my head down and my trap shut, especially when she got a bit maggoty. But boy, a couple of times there this week, Gene, she really got my back up! It didn't matter what I said, I couldn't win!

I rang her the other day and said, 'Look, Sonya, if you're not feeling a hundred per cent, I'll come over and run your messages for you.'

You know what she said in that voice of hers that freezes magpies in mid-air? 'No thanks, I'll take care of what I need to do.'

'All right,' I said, 'you don't have to be like that! I was only offering to help because you were crook. I'll go away.'

'You just worry about yourself,' she said.

The way she put it I was about to suggest she open a window at her end because the condescension must have been fogging up all the windows.

I said, 'I'd wish you'd told me just to look after myself last week when I filled in for you at the op shop when you had to go to the Doctor's.'

'You didn't have to do it.'

'No, I didn't, but you asked me to, so I did.'

I thought to myself, 'Bugger it, she can run her own messages, if she's going to be like that.'

So, anyway, I'm down the post office about an hour later and I run into Thelma Hopgood, with a list as long as her arm, doing all your mum's messages for her. Not only that, Thelma ticks me off for not helping your mum when she's sick!

That was it, I'd had enough, so I flew around to your mum's joint and jeez, I was wild. Had to calm myself down on the porch before I rang the bell because I thought I'd be likely to throw a seven, the way I was feeling – especially without my tablets.

So I explained I'd run into Thelma and said, 'Look here, Sonya. I'm fed up with this business. Make up your mind; if you don't want me around, that's fine, but I'm buggered if I'm going to feel like a feather duster one minute and a bloody rooster the next. It's as simple as that.' Jeez, I was cranky!

'What are you going on about, you silly dill?' she said.

I said, 'Well, one minute you want me around, the next you make me feel as useless as a bloody ashtray on a motorbike. Fair dinkum!'

I don't like raising my voice to anyone, let alone your mum, but as far as I'm concerned, in the last couple of weeks Gene, your mum has really gone over the Plimsoll line.

I said to her, 'Look, Sonya, I just want to know where I stand.'

'What a lot of tripe!' she said.

'It's not tripe!'

'It is tripe!'

'No, it's not!' I said.

'Yes, it is tripe,' says your mum.

It went on like this for an hour or so.

'Don't raise your voice at me, Roly Parks!'

'I'm not raising my voice at you.'

'You're raising your voice!'

'No I'm not!'

'You are!'

'I'm not!'

'Listen to you!'

'Listen to *you*!'

'You raised it first.'

'You did!'

'No. I. Did. Not!'

'Oh, yes. You. Did!'

'Did not.'

'Did so.'

I finally said to her, 'Look, Sonya, for God's sake, what's getting on your goat? Why are you dark on me?'

'You know why. You want to divorce me, don't you?' she says.

'I want to *what*?'

'Divorce me.'

'For crying out loud Sonya, who said anything about a divorce? Did I say that?'

'No, you didn't.'

'I didn't?'

'No,' she said, 'you didn't, not in as many words.'

'Well, for God's sake. What makes you think I want one?'

'Because you took the records,' she said.

'I took what?'

'The records.'

'What records?' I said.

'All the James Last and Klaus Wunderlich albums we had!'

'Yes, I took them to listen to. So?'

'So, you never gave them back.'

'I haven't finished listening to them,' I said.

'Well, why didn't you tell me that? Why didn't you tell me that was why you didn't give them back?'

'Maybe it was because I didn't know that I had to!'

'Well you should have!'

'Why?'

You know what your mum said, Gene? She said, 'Because I thought you were splitting up all the stuff we owned so you could divorce me.'

I give up. Can you work out the logic of that, Gene? If you can, write and let me know will you? It's got me completely buggered.

Anyway, I pulled up stumps after that, went home and I rang your sister Sharon to see if she could throw some light on the matter. She went and consulted the *I Ching* oracle thing she reads. It said, 'You cannot solve your problems alone. Swallow your pride and seek aid. Choose the right source for this aid and all will be well.'

So I rang my mate Milton and we went down the pub.

Keep all this under your hat though, won't you? Your mum's running out of material at the marriage counsellor's and the last thing I want to do is top up her tank with more petrol.

Give my regards to Ahmed. I hope you're both well and write soon.

Lots of love,
Your dad

SPUD TURNER
& THE AMAZING ARTHUR

Kalangadoo, Monday

Dear Gene,

How are you son? You winning?

Not much to report. Milton and I went to see an old mate of mine perform at the Horny Stallion Bistro over there in Millicent.

I don't know if you'd remember The Amazing Arthur, the facial illusionist from Penola? Anyway, Arthur was head-lining the cabaret night so we booked a dinner and show.

Arthur has been working up at the Gold Coast at one of those resort-type places for the last year and cleaning up, so he told us. Ever since he added the penguin into his act, he has never looked back. It was a brilliant idea – who would have thought of combining facial illusion with a talking animal act? I can't think of too many performers who'd change their act that dramatically. Not at the age of 70 after 60 years in the business! Just shows you the talent of some people.

I mean, Arthur was always a very good ventriloquist but he never did it on stage. Arthur reckoned there were blokes better at it, that's why he stuck to his facial illusions. I suppose when you have double joints in your face, you're not going to have a lot of competition, are you? That's why he did so well.

But like everything, the public eventually tires of you. That's what happened to Arthur; he couldn't get arrested with his act for nearly ten years. Still, to his credit he never gave up and never chucked in the towel. Arthur was telling me about it the other night after the show.

'I knew I needed a new act, Roly, and had to find a new idea, but for the life of me, I couldn't think what. Then one night I was watching the telly and that old show with the talking horse, *Mr Ed*, came on and I thought to myself, that's it! That's the gimmick! What I need is a real horse on stage in place of the ventriloquist's dummy.

'It was a pretty good idea at the time, but when the grog wore off in the morning I realised that carting a horse around the countryside was a bit high maintenance.'

I can see his problem, Gene. As Arthur said to me, 'Even if you got lucky and could have trained a horse to open its mouth when you wanted it to on stage, the RSL Club would think you were off your lolly!'

And that was what happened. Arthur rang a few clubs he'd played at to see if there was any interest and they hung up on him. Thought he was crackers. Anyway, not one to let failure get in the way of a good idea, Arthur thinks 'right idea, wrong size!'

So you know what he does, Gene? He goes out the next day and buys a penguin! God knows from where or whom. But Arthur buys it and takes it to this animal trainer he knows on the Gold Coast and the bloke shows him how he can train this penguin to be his ventriloquist's dummy. It took him a year.

Gene, you have to see this penguin and Arthur together – you'd wet yourself. Funny? The penguin is sensational! I mean, I don't know if you can imagine it; here you have Arthur doing his facial contortion routine – which is pretty bloody funny for starters – twisting his face up to look like a wombat or whatever, then in the middle of the act, out waddles this penguin, it climbs up a little ladder and then plonks herself on a pedestal next to Arthur.

The penguin opens her mouth and says, 'I know a doctor who can fix that!' Then as everyone is laughing, the penguin turns to the audience and says, 'It's true! Trust me, I used to be one!'

I tell you, Gene. I mean, I've seen ventriloquist acts before, but Arthur and that penguin – you'd swear the penguin is really talking! They're billed as 'The Amazing Arthur & Penelope the Talking Penguin'. I don't think I've ever come across a cabaret act like it, and I've seen a few. They're booked out for a year and a half, so Arthur reckons.

Good on him eh? Not bad for a facial illusionist from Penola and a penguin from the Gold Coast. Goes to show you, Gene: in this business, never give up.

By the way, speaking of never giving up, did I tell you that Pearl La Monde's come out of retirement again? You remember the jazz singer Pearl La Monde from when you were young? You used to like her dresses. Well, Spud Turner, our agent who runs Spud Turner's International Class Acts, is putting together another series of 'farewell' concerts for Pearl. They kick off with a couple of nights at the Horny Stallion in Millicent, then a few nights at Merino's Nightclub over in Penola.

I was talking to Spud the other night about it. He says Pearl is off the grog and the valium and is singing better than ever. Apparently the therapy has gone well and she's not as bitter as she used to be. Which is good, isn't it? It was a shame the way Pearl went in the end – blaming Spud for not making her the big star she thought she should have been. Trouble was, Pearl always saw herself as someone who could have made it big time at the clubs in Sydney.

I think not getting the job singing on the cruise ship to the Pacific sort of tipped her over the edge artistically, you know. After that, she hit the plonk in a big way and her career went downhill. So it's beaut that she's back.

Speaking of Spud Turner, it's his fiftieth anniversary in the business this year. That's the other reason Pearl has come out of retirement. She's going to sing at his celebrations in a couple of weeks. So are your mum and me of course; we'd been with Spud for 30 years. He's had an incredible career the old Spud, especially when you consider who he started his booking agency with. The first act he booked was old Merton Mathews the close-up magician – he's dead now of course, Merton.

Then he had Molly what's-her-name, the belly dancer from Penola, she's gone too I think. Then there was the Swinging Samuel Sisters, the singing trapeze act. Sad the way they went – tragic – and of course, Clarrie Simms and his International Orchestra got their start with Spud.

So, he's come a long way since those days. I was looking at who he's got on the books at the moment and there are tap dancers, singers, clowns and fire-eaters. Spud runs the Bucking Bull down at the Horny Stallion and he's got Trevor the Sheep Juggling Act from Port McDonald, and Shirley the Lingerie Artiste down at the motel dining room works for him.

Spud also manages the jelly wrestling on Thursday night at Merino's, and if you want a Father Christmas in this neck of the woods, well I think he's got that business sewn up as well. Spud was always a great spotter of emerging talent.

Not everyone can do it. I remember when he first took on The Amazing Arthur, I said 'Spud, I'm not sure how a joker pulling silly faces all night is going to go down here. I mean you can go down the pub and see old Clem Baxter do that after he's had a couple.' I was very wrong.

Anyway, I had better go. Got to think about what your mum and I might do for Spud's celebration.

Give my regards to Ahmed and write soon.

Lots of love,
Your dad

ESCAPE FROM STALAG 17
& LOSING KELVIN

Kalangadoo, Monday

Dear Gene,

How are you son?

Not bad myself, though I had a bit of an accident last weekend. I tripped over Milton's bloody cat in the laundry and you've got no idea what I did to myself.

Ended up in hospital having a skin graft – I got 36 stitches in my leg. I've been over at Mount Gambier in Stalag 17 all week, under the careless eye of old Doc Wilson and his stormtroopers. Only got home this morning.

Wilson wanted me to stay in for another week, but there was no way I was doing that. He only wants me in there so he can inflict pain on me, the old bugger. I think he secretly likes seeing me suffer; seeing me in pain gives him some sort of warped pleasure.

Your mum dropped in to see me while I was there. She was visiting your aunt Gwennie in the religious trauma unit and she'd heard I hurt myself and decided to pop in and tell me I was a silly old bugger who ought to look where he's going next time. Just the sort of warm compassion you need when in a recovery ward with a leg that looks like a sewing machine's attacked it.

Anyway, in the end I pulled a swiftie on Doc Wilson. I waited until the old bugger went off duty and a younger doctor replaced him on his rounds. The young doctor comes in to check on me and asks how I'm feeling. I told him that I was worried sick about my dog, Benaud, and my cocky, Harvey, who was 27 years old in July, and explained that there wasn't anyone at home to feed them. I added that if I didn't get home that night they might be dead by the morning, if they weren't that way already.

Boy did he come in on the grouter! 'Oh,' he said, looking at me with great concern, 'do you think you are OK to go home?'

'Oh yes,' I said, 'I'm fine but I am very worried about my animals.'

'It sounds like you'd better go,' he said and then signed me out while I was trying to keep a straight face.

I rang Milton – whose idea it was originally – so Milton came and picked me up and half an hour later we were having a beer around the fire at home.

He knows how to escape from a hospital that Milton. He's a genius that boy, I tell you.

Best part about it was that I'd had a bet with the night sister that I'd be out of there before she was off duty. So not only did I get out, but I took $10 off 'Broomhilda the Nazi' – which is always a victory for the people I reckon. She's a cruel woman that night sister, Gene, she's a shocker. I don't know how they let her alone with patients. God, if we were animals, you'd call in the RSPCA and lay charges against her!

Anyway, I'm back home now, I'm all right, still a bit woozy, but she'll be Jake. Milton's looking after me with the meals and stuff and your sister Sharon is doing my washing and running a few messages for me. I should be OK in a few days. I damn well better be — Snowy Thompson's son, Kelvin, is getting married on Saturday and I'm the Master of Ceremonies.

You remember Snowy? Of course you do! Snowy Thompson lives down there on Railway Crescent. Snowy's wife runs the Shell station in town and Snow's got the inter-state trucking concern here. His dad, old Clem Thompson, and me were good mates for years, right up until he died.

Snowy and Pam have brought Kelvin up well you know. It wasn't easy either; Snowy's first wife ran off and left him with Kelvin when he was only 18 months old. Just took off one night and he never saw her again.

I said to Snowy when he told me, 'Eighteen months old! Who looked after him?'

'I did. I had to, what else could I do?' he said.

'How did you manage that?' I said. 'Weren't you driving semi-trailers interstate?'

'Well yeah, but there was no one to look after him was there? I had to take the little bugger with me.'

'Get away,' I said. 'How did you get on?'

'Well, the kid could have had me up for assault with a deadly weapon while I learned how to operate the nappies, but he survived. We got there in the end.'

'You changed his nappies on the road?'

'You changed them when they needed changing, mate, on the road or in the truck. I changed most of them in men's rooms at petrol stations,' he said.

His wife Pam was telling me that Snowy and young Kelvin became a legend on the road there for a while. Snowy was a bit of a folk hero, especially among the truckies' girlfriends and wives. He got a lot of brownie points from the women for taking the kid on the way he did. The truckies' wives and girlfriends used to help out too. Snowy got this network going and there wasn't a town where he couldn't drop off nappies to get washed or have Kelvin looked after if he got sick, which is how Pam met Snowy.

As she said to me, 'Any bloke who could do what Snowy had done was going to do me, so I married him.'

Pam was saying that at one stage Snowy lost Kelvin on one of his trips. Well, he didn't lose Kelvin as such – he just misplaced him.

What happened was Snowy had been crisscrossing the country in the semi and in one particularly hectic week he had gone from Sydney to Adelaide, down to Melbourne and back up to Adelaide again. Kelvin was still a bub at this stage and he'd got a bit crook, so Snowy arranged for him to be left with one of the truckies' wives in Ararat on the way to Adelaide.

When Snowy finished his run in Adelaide he got on the turps one night and then he gets crook himself. A couple of days later he comes good, but when he tries to remember who he'd left Kelvin with, for the life of him he can't recall where it was or with whom. So Snowy phones a few people he thinks might have him, but no luck.

Snowy knows Kelvin is all right, but he is starting to panic a bit, so he hops in the semi and heads back to Sydney thinking he might remember along the way where

Kelvin is. Anyway, Snowy gets to Murray Bridge and pulls into the Shell service station for a feed and as he walks into the café, five big truckies jump up and threaten to knock his block off for abandoning his kid with Bob Toohey's girlfriend in Ararat. That's how he found out where Kelvin was.

The truckies had got really protective of Kelvin, so Pam was saying. They were sort of like his road uncles; they were great big sooks when it came to Kelvin.

That was 26 years ago and now Kelvin is getting married himself and, isn't it funny, Kelvin is marrying Bob Toohey's youngest girl, Charlene. You wouldn't read about it, would you?

Anyway, I better go, I've got to write something to say at the wedding reception. It's going to be a big turnout apparently. As Pam was saying, you wouldn't want to be shipping something interstate on a semi this weekend; you'd be pushing your luck to find a truck, let alone a driver.

Give my regards to Ahmed and write soon.

Lots of love,
Your dad

SNOWY'S WEDDING NIGHT
PUNCH-UP

Kalangadoo, Monday

Dear Gene,

How are you son? You winning?

I'm pretty good myself, been a bit busy — I was the MC on Saturday at Snowy Thompson's young lad Kelvin's wedding. It went off well in the end but they had a few problems, unfortunately.

For some reason Snowy and Pam invited the three Wilson boys along to the wedding, so it was a lay-down misère a fight was going to break out at some stage. It was just a shame it had to start in the church during the ceremony.

Still, it shouldn't have surprised anyone. You know what the Wilson boys are like; they've got the kangaroos loose in the top paddock, that lot. I mean, they're real idiots, the Wilson boys.

So anyway, the ceremony is going along and then it gets to the part where Father Ryan asks if there is anyone present who thinks the pair shouldn't be husband and wife. And what happens? Stupid bloody Craig Wilson has to yell out at the top of his voice, 'Yeah, me. She's my wife!' and he and his brothers start laughing their silly heads off.

Gene, you can imagine what happened from here. I mean, half the interstate trucking fraternity is there and they know Charlene wasn't married to anyone else. So a couple of these big blokes grab hold of Craig Wilson and job him then and there on the spot. This sets off the other two idiot brothers, Mick and Wayne, who start throwing punches at anyone who comes near them and we have the wild west on our hands. It was on for young and old.

Snowy's wife Pam starts belting Craig's girlfriend over the head with her bag, Wayne Wilson's wife starts kicking a few truckies and Father Ryan, the poor old bugger, is looking like he wants the heavens to open and beam him up.

Eventually the congregation managed to get hold of the Wilson boys and turf them outside the church, where the local walloper arrests the Wilsons and calls for a divvy-van to take them away. After this, we all go back inside the church and Father Ryan marries the two of them as quick as he could.

It was all a bit of a shame really, it could have ruined the whole day. Clarrie Sims, who did the music at the turn afterwards, said to me, 'You expect a blue at a wedding, don't you? I mean, a wedding is not a wedding without some joker getting upset over his girlfriend dancing with another bloke or whatever.' Still, as Clarrie pointed out, he's seen plenty of blues at turns but he's never seen one *before* the turn.

Anyway, the wedding reception went off as quiet as buggery — never seen so many well-behaved people.

Neither had Clarrie and he has played at something like 2000 of them.

Well Gene, I better choof off. I've got to pop down to Spud Turner's office and pick up a couple of cheques from the ABC that have been overdue since the year before last.

Give my regards to Ahmed and write soon.

Lots of love,
Your dad

BURYING BULL DEVINE

Port Adelaide, Thursday

Dear Gene,

How are you son?

I'm all right – sort of. It's been a bit of a sad week for us over here. My old mate Bull Devine passed away last Thursday, that's why I'm here in Adelaide for the funeral.

Strange how it happened too; he died suddenly of a heart attack. Lorne and him were about to leave to go to the bingo apparently and he popped into the toilet before they left and anyway, he dropped dead on the toot. Just like that. Least he went quickly, though I don't know if I'd want to be called to my maker while I'm sitting on the throne.

I guess it doesn't matter does it? When your number is up your number is up I suppose, it doesn't matter where it happens. Still, I'd like to at least be in my pyjamas and in bed if possible, it's less embarrassing if you know what I mean. But then it was typical of Bull to drop dead in the lavatory – he was always doing the unexpected.

Anyway, they held the funeral on Monday and we buried him the day before yesterday in the river of Port Adelaide. Well, we didn't actually bury him, he was cremated and wanted his ashes scattered down the river where he grew up.

So, Lorne asked Jack Sampson, Shagger Price and myself to do the honours, but I tell you what, we had a bugger of a time getting rid of him. I mean, looking back on it, you shouldn't laugh I know, but even Bull would've laughed if he'd been there. Well, he was there. I mean if Bull was there and he was alive, he would have wet himself.

What happened was, we get down to the Port with Bull in the box in the back of Shagger's car, then we pick up the dinghy we were renting down at the wharf and off we go. Well of course, it was just our luck that it's blowing a bloody gale that day and the damn dinghy's tipping up and down all over the place. Jack and I are trying to keep the bloody boat upright while Shagger is trying to toss Bull's ashes in. Trouble is every time Shagger scatters a bit of Bull into Port River, a bit of Bull blows back at us, all over our coats and in our hair.

We all tried to be a bit solemn, after all it was sad, but I tell you what, I'm afraid when some of the ashes blew back on us and Jack, the silly bugger, turned to me and said, 'Hey, Roly, I think Bull's having second thoughts, I think he wants to come home with us', well that did it. I mean, laugh, the three of us, I tell you, how we kept the bloody dinghy upright has still got me beat.

We calmed down eventually. We had to, it was getting dark and we still had half of Bull's ashes in the damn box.

Anyway, we put our heads together and decided that given the way the wind was carrying on, the only way we were going to get rid of Bull completely was to chuck the box with the ashes into the river, which is what we did.

That was all right until we got home and told Lorne what we'd done and she got really upset. Apparently, Lorne wanted to keep the box and stick it on the mantelpiece above the fire in memory of Bull. Well we didn't know that, did we?

Anyway, the upshot was that the three of us had to go and hire the dinghy again the next morning and try and find the bloody box. Talk about three lads getting themselves into trouble. It must have been just after dawn when we started looking for the damn thing. Anyway, we couldn't have been there more than ten minutes when out of the blue the bloody police launch pulls up alongside us and wants to know what we're up to.

Not a surprise; three blokes in a dinghy with one fishing rod among them probably looked a bit suspicious, especially at that time of the morning. And of course, silly bloody Jack didn't help, he tells the wallopers we're looking for a box our mate was in when we got rid of him the day before.

It was only after the wallopers got Lorne on the phone to verify the story that they let us go. Bull would have been up there laughing his silly damn head off I reckon.

Anyway, it's sad him going. I'm going to miss Bull, but still, it's nice knowing he's in the Port River. At least next time I'm over in Adelaide I can wander down to the Port and know the old bugger's in there somewhere, chatting away to the fish no doubt.

Anyway, I had better get going, I've got to catch the bus back to Kalangadoo tonight and Jack, Shagger and I are going up to the hospital to see Lionel Cameron before I leave. Lionel's a bit crook and we're going to cheer him up a bit. As Jack said, we don't want to be renting that bloody dinghy again for a while.

Give my regards to Ahmed and write when you can.

Lots of love,
Your dad

JACK SMILLETT-WHINGER

Kalangadoo, Monday

Dear Gene,

How are you son? You winning? Keeping the dingoes off the front step? That's the shot.

Thanks for ringing me during the week, you didn't have to do that Gene. It must cost you a fortune ringing up from London but I really enjoyed the chat.

The trouble is, there's not a lot of people you can talk to these days about stuff that's sort of personal like that. What am I saying? There's not a lot of people you can talk to about anything these days.

There used to be. People now are too busy to give you the time of day. Either that or they'll only listen to you a minute and then they'll start talking to you about their problems. Funny when that happens, it becomes like a competition to see who has got the worst problems.

Speaking of which, 'Whingeing' Jack Smillett died this week. Now, Jack was like that; 'King of the Whinge' we used to call him. Do you remember Jack? He lived about three doors up from your mum's. Jack was the caretaker up at the cemetery for years.

Now he's dead, he's got nothing much to complain about anymore, thank God. But seriously, Gene, Jack would had to have been the biggest whinger I ever met in my life. He was like those jokers who would ask you 'how are you going?' only so they could get a right of reply.

You'd be sitting in the pub having a schooner and in would come Jack looking as miserable as a shag on the rock and you'd try not to ask him how he was getting on because that was his cue to tell you how crook things were in his life. Didn't matter how you avoided asking him how he was, Jack could always find a way to turn a discussion into a whinge about something. Then you'd be sitting there for two hours listening to the misery. The worst part was half of Jack's problems he'd make up and the other half happened to him 20 years before and he was still going on about it.

If he wasn't whingeing about his bad luck in his personal life, it'd be about what the council wasn't doing or how someone had put his nose out of joint over something or other. If whingeing was an Olympic event, Jack could have bored for his country.

I think Jack's whingeing problem had a lot to do with his job, just quietly. You don't get a lot of fun in your life wandering around gravesites five days a week. You know, you get up in the morning feeling on top of the world, you'd have a cup of tea and then have to go and bury someone, probably someone you know. And he buried a few people in his time Jack; I know, because when he wasn't talking about his problems he talked about who he had buried that week, how the funeral had gone, who was there, that sort of thing.

It would really get on my quince after a while. I'd be sitting around having a beer and Jack would be yakking on about the cemetery and its history and you'd say to him, 'For God's sake Jack, will you stop rabbiting on about the bloody cemetery, I'll have plenty of time to think about the cemetery when I'm up there!'

I think that's the problem when your job becomes your life, which it did in Jack's case.

He even travelled overseas to look at them. Oh, yeah, Jack and his wife Dot would go overseas every November to look at mausoleums, acropolises and other famous cemeteries. Not too many cemeteries in Europe Jack and Dot hadn't seen. Trust me, I know. One of the most depressing nights of your life was when Jack and Dot returned and put on a slide night showing slides from one of their cemetery tours. Hell, you'd avoid that invitation like the plague. Not as boring as Ethel and Jim Bennett's slide nights mind you, but a hell of a lot more depressing, that's for sure.

It was odd when Jack died last week. At the funeral, everyone reckoned it was the first time anyone had seen a smile on Jack's face. Your mother reckoned it was because he had finally got away from his wife. I remember saying to your mum, 'Sonya, that's not very nice.' 'No, it's not,' she said, 'but it's true.'

Your mum never liked Dot Smillett, of course. In fact, to be honest, nobody liked Dot Smillett all that much – it was true, she was hard to like. Not that you wouldn't try to like her, but it didn't seem to matter what you did, you would always end up walking away saying, 'Bugger it, I don't really like her.'

I don't know what it was about Dot, I think she was just mean. She had a mean soul; you know how the old saying goes, 'She was so mean if a blowfly landed in the sugar she'd shake its legs before she killed it.' That's Dot Smillett.

In the early days before we stopped inviting them around, Jack and Dot would come for dinner and you'd say, 'Dot would you like a cup of tea?' and she'd say, 'Not now thanks very much. I would have liked one earlier, but I'll be all right, I'll wait until I get home.'

Or you'd be making lunch and she'd always find a reason why she couldn't eat it, no matter what it was. 'Thanks very much, but I can't eat that, Doctor Wilson says it's bad for me.'

'Well, we'll make something else, what would you like?' we ask. 'Don't worry about me, Sonya, you eat, I'll just sit here. I'll eat when I get home.'

And of course, she never helped with the dishes either. 'Well, I never ate,' I once heard her say to her husband, 'why should I do the dishes?'

When Dot had to be moved into the nursing home she really hit her straps; she drove the nurses mad. I think Dot Smillett was the first person in medical history to get expelled from a nursing home – they asked her to leave.

She's over at the Mary MacKillop Nursing Home in Penola these days, driving the nuns there to drink apparently. I didn't say that by the way, Father Ryan did.

'Dot's with us to test the faith,' he said.

Dot Smillett would have even tested Mary MacKillop's faith if you ask me.

Anyway Gene, I'd better stop whingeing about Jack and Dot. Give my regards to Ahmed and write soon.

Lots of love,
Your dad

SAPPER HOSKINGS'S WILL

Kalangadoo, Monday

Dear Gene,

How are you son? How's it all going?

I got your letter this morning by the way. That's beaut news about you buying the apartment with Ahmed!

Gene, you never mentioned about needing any money towards it – I don't know how you are off in that department and I haven't got a lot stashed away, but if you need what I have got, don't not ask just because you're not sure if you should ask or not.

I don't know if I'm explaining myself all that well. What I'm saying, Gene, is if you need a bit of a hand, give me a hoy. I mean you're going to get it all in the end anyway, so you might as well have it now – I said this to your sister Sharon only the other day.

Your mum and I have been having a bit of a chat about wills and I know you don't like talking about it, but at some stage you have to sort out who is going to get what – you can't do it after you've carked it, can you? You don't want it to become a problem for anyone so it's better to sort it out beforehand so everyone knows what's what.

Not everyone does of course, and look what happens; the angels come and get you and the last breath is hardly out of your body before the bloody family starts fighting each other over the booty.

I've seen it happen, Gene, it happens too often. Do you remember my old mate Sapper Hoskings from Adelaide? His ashes are up there in a box at Centennial Park. I mean Sapper's a bloody good example. Poor old bugger, he came back from the war and worked himself to death and when he died you should have seen the carry-on Gene; a couple of his family members were like animals.

You see, Sapper had come into quite a bit of dough-re-mi there in the sixties when he struck Tatts. Sapper, who had never had any dough in his life, became the biggest touch in town after winning Tatts – making friends overnight, he was. His family were the worst.

Talk about in for a penny, in for a pound. And this was *after* Sapper had already bought them a house each and set them all up. It never stopped them though; if they'd want a new lounge suite or something, they'd get on the blower to the old man and of course, Sapper never learned to say no.

Of course, Sapper didn't care about money, so he'd always roll over and let them have it.

A few of his old mates – me, Bull Devine and Shagger Price – were getting a bit worried that Sapper was going to end up with nothing again, especially at the rate of knots his money was disappearing.

Anyway, the three of us had a bit of a word to Sapper and convinced him to get a financial adviser to help him invest what was left.

Sapper thought that this was a beaut idea because all he wanted was a bit of money every week to put on the races and have a drink and feed. His wife, Narelle, had passed on so he only had himself to look after.

Anyway, he gets some financial advice and of course, the money supply dries up and his family drop him like a hotcake. They stopped going around to see him and hardly called to say hello anymore, apart from when it was getting close to Christmas or their birthdays, just to remind him to buy them something in case he'd forgotten. With the exception of his daughter, Meredith, it was bloody terrible the way they treated him. Funny what greed and money does to some people.

But Sapper, who wasn't stupid by a long shot, looked at the way his sons were carrying on but didn't say anything. A few years later when he wrote his will, that's when the chickens really came home to roost.

Boy, did he stitch them up good and proper. I know, I was there the day Sapper's will was read out by his executor. Me, Bull Devine and Shagger Price were all there.

We all knew Sapper had a bloody good sense of humour; he was one of the funniest buggers I've ever come across. Not funny in an obvious sort of way, Sapper's humour was subtle. Well, he turned it into an art form if the will was any indication.

There was the family sitting around in the room when the executor starts reading Sapper's last will and testament.

Well, Shagger looked at me, I looked at Bull and then none of us could look at each other after that for fear of laughing – Sapper had got back at the buggers! I can remember it as if it was yesterday.

The executor started: 'To my eldest son Robert, I leave my good hammer and a box of nails. This is in case something falls off the house I bought you and you need to repair it. You're not getting any of my money because you've had enough already and I promised your dead mother I wouldn't spoil you.' Well, you should have seen the look on Robert's face when the executor read that out – he went white. I can still see his jaw dropping.

And here's what he left his other son: 'To my son Trevor, I bequeath my only pick and shovel to use in the garden of the house I bought for you, and you're not getting any money either for the same reasons as your older brother.' Well, I remember Trevor's wife bursting out crying at that stage and running out of the room.

Well, Shagger, Bull and I had to go to the toilet at this point because Shagger got the giggles and that started Bull and me off and it was getting bloody embarrassing. Talk about laugh; when we got outside the room, dearie me, I thought we were all going to have coronaries.

The upshot of it all was that Sapper left his car, house and quite a bit of cash to his daughter, Meredith, because: 'My darling daughter, you never asked me for a thing, but you gave me a hell of a lot.'

To fix his boys good and proper, he left all his shares, investments and quite a bit of moolah to his sons' children to be put in trust until they turned sixteen. The only catch was if any of them joined the armed forces, they would lose the lot; the money would go instead to Legacy. Legacy look after war widows, Gene, they're a good mob.

Sapper also left a couple of thousand for Bull, Shagger and me to have a wake and put a bet on the Melbourne Cup every year until we all passed on. If we won any money, we had to spend it shouting rounds down at the RSL.

Sapper also put $5000 aside for legal fees to be used when Trevor and Robert went to court to contest his will – which they did of course Gene, and lost.

He was a funny bugger, Sapper.

Anyway, I had better go. Behave yourselves you two, and write and let me know if you do need some money – I won't write you out of the will if you do!

Give my love to Ahmed and write soon.

Lots of love,
Your dad

BLUEY DODSON & FRED ALDRIDGE

Kalangadoo, Monday

Dear Gene,

How are you son? You winning?

I'm pretty good myself. Haven't got much to tell you, really.

Oh, I got a letter from me old mate Bluey Dodson in Adelaide. You remember Bluey? Well, he's out of hospital. Not that that's all that remarkable, except they'd given Bluey a week to live 12 months ago.

We didn't take much notice of the doctors at the time because we know Bluey – he's been given up for dead a few times in his career, the old Blue. The first time was in 1941 when he went down on the HMAS *Perth* in the Java Sea. Bluey survived that, then the Japanese got hold of him and slung him in a POW camp after which they tossed him on the Burma Railway.

If that wasn't enough, he was then shipped off to Nagasaki in Japan to work in the salt mines and the Yanks dropped an atomic bomb on the place. He survived that as well!

So he's got to do a lot more than die before you can pronounce Bluey Dodson dead, that's for sure. He's like a stayer in the Melbourne Cup.

It's a bit of a sad time for Bluey though; one of his close mates didn't stay the distance. Bluey was telling me in the letter that Fred Aldridge passed on this week. I never knew Fred personally, but I knew a lot about him.

He was a walloper, retired now of course. Well, I mean he was retired before he...well, before he really retired – before he died, I mean.

Typical of Bluey to have a copper for a mate. He hated the coppers all his life and ends up becoming close mates with one! Bluey hated anything in a uniform; he hated authority and anyone who tried to tell him what to do. He'd do anything to stick it up the authorities, Blue. It became a thing with him, he went looking for it.

That's how he met Fred Aldridge the copper – it was funny how it happened.

After the war, Bluey couldn't hold down a job, you see, he used to get bored easily. Having a real job was all a bit too routine for him I think. He used to say to me that after surviving all the things he did during the war, having a nine-to-five job where your life wasn't in danger was something he couldn't do.

Oh, he tried a few things, but I think the most dangerous life ever got for him was when he married Minnie Dawkins, who used to run the British Hotel in Port Adelaide.

Anyway, Minnie introduced him to an SP bookie and that's what he became. It's what Bluey did in the pubs around the port for 25 years and he never ever got caught. There was a reason, of course, which I'll tell you later on.

Now, being an SP bookie wasn't all that dangerous but it meant he could pit himself against the system, you know, the coppers. He did pretty well at it. Did bloody well in fact. He used to drive the wallopers mad because they knew what he was doing but there was nothing much they could do about it. They would try – try setting him up for a bet – but Bluey could smell a walloper the moment one stepped in the pub door.

Anyway, that's how he became mates with Fred Aldridge years later because Fred was a copper down the Port and Fred knew Bluey was an SP bookie. He'd been trying to book him for 20 years or more.

When Fred Aldridge finally retired from the force, it must have bugged the hell out of him how Blue had got away with it all those years. He might have known what Bluey was doing, but for the life of him he never knew how he was doing it. So about a year after he's left the force, Bluey gets a phone call. It's from Fred Aldridge who asks Blue if he could come and see him.

So Blue meets Fred at the British, one of the scenes of the crime, and while they are having a few drinks Fred says, 'Listen, Blue, I know you were running the books in the Port but I'm getting on, pal, and I've got to know how you did it. It's driving me crazy. I've got to know. I can't go to my grave not knowing.'

'I thought you knew,' says Blue, 'thought you were just going easy on a returned soldier!'

'Like bloody hell I would have gone easy on you,' says Fred. 'If I could have worked it out, I would have chucked you in the clink quicker than look at you.'

'You'd dob me in if I told you now!' says Bluey.

'I'll bloody kill you if you don't tell me!' says Fred. 'On my honour, Bluey, the secret dies with me – I promise!'

Well, Fred Aldridge was the only copper Bluey ever had time for. He had seen Fred operate around the Port and he never got rough with anyone or big-noted himself and was always polite. So Bluey decided to give Fred the drum.

'Well,' he said, 'when I was in the POW camps and on the railway, I had this idea that one day I might want to write a book about the people in the camps. Problem was there was no paper or pens to write anything down, so I trained myself over those years in prison to remember faces. If I remembered the face I could recall the event. I might forget a name in seconds, but a face and the event – never!'

The retired walloper just looked at Bluey in disbelief. 'Bugger me dead! You never wrote the bets down? You remembered the face – you remembered the bet! No wonder we could never bloody nick you! Bloody hell!' said Fred. 'You don't have to be dead to be stiff, do you?!'

'No,' says Bluey, 'that's what I said when the Yanks dropped the bomb on us!'

Well, Bluey and Fred became good mates after that. I think they developed a mutual respect, as you'd expect.

Anyway, Fred passed on this week...how did I get onto that? Not sure, sorry Gene, I didn't mean to bore you. I better go anyway.

Write soon.

Lots of love,
Your dad

RUBY CUNNINGHAM

Kalangadoo, Monday

Dear Gene,

How are you son? All right?

I don't know if your mum wrote and told you about the big crash here in town on Tuesday morning or not.

What happened was the idiot local council down here decided to remove all the stop signs in town and put in roundabouts. Ridiculous idea. Some of the oldies in town have enough trouble driving their car these days, let alone trying to steer themselves around bloody roundabouts! Especially if they've got a trailer on the back.

Anyway, the stupid council decide to stick one in at the corner of Abattoir Street and Railway Crescent, you see. The problem was they forgot to tell Snowy Thompson. You remember Snowy, he runs the interstate trucking business here. His wife Pam used to be a dancer and now runs the local garage.

So anyway, Snowy is up in Wagga all last week, picking up some cattle. He arrives back in town last Tuesday morning and nobody has told him that the stop sign had gone and that they'd put in the roundabout.

Now, everyone knows Snowy never takes any notice of the stop signs in town anyway, let alone at 2 am in the morning. Crikey! If you see Snowy Thompson's truck coming through town at that hour of the morning, you get out of the bloody way!

So here comes Snowy hurtling down Railway Crescent. He gets to the corner of Abattoir Street and Railway Crescent where the stop sign used to be and drives himself and 200 head of prime beef right over the top of the roundabout.

I didn't hear the crash myself, but poor old Ruby Cunningham certainly did – it is a bit hard to miss a semi-trailer crashing through your front fence and making its way into your bedroom at two o'clock in the morning, I suppose.

No one was hurt, thank God. According to the police, Ruby passed out for a while and when she come to, there was cattle all over the garden and Snowy with his head stuck out the truck window asking her if she had a cold beer in the fridge.

As Father Ryan said to me in the street the next day, 'I think it was God's will that Ruby Cunningham wasn't meant to die from being run over by a semi-trailer in her bedroom.'

I think Father Ryan has a point. Anyway, Ruby says she's going to sue the local council for attempted murder – which, given that she was dead against the roundabout going up in the first place, is probably fair enough.

I better choof off. I'm going over to Milton's for a card game and am going to try and recover some of your inheritance I lost last time.

Give my regards to Ahmed – I hope you're both well. Write soon.

Lots of love,
Your dad

A CHAT WITH THE
GRAND-DAUGHTER

Kalangadoo, Monday

Dear Gene,

How are you son? Keeping the dingoes off the front step
are you?

I'm all right myself in a manner of speaking – I'm alive.
That's always a victory, waking up and finding the engine
is still ticking over.

I've had a pretty good week actually; well, after the
last few weeks even a really bad week is a bloody good
week. I've been a bit busy to tell you the truth. Your sister
Sharon has gone up north to stay with a friend and to
try and sort a few things out about the marriage business,
so I've been helping out looking after young Tracey and
Stephen over at Sharon's place. Your mum has done half
the week and I've done the other half.

I don't know, I must be getting a bit old or something,
but I'm buggered if I can understand teenagers these
days. Tracey and Stephen are beaut kids and I love them
of course, but some of the music they play Gene. I said
to them, 'That's not bloody music, that's an assault on

your brain – put on some Frank Sinatra, or someone who can sing!'

'Who?' they said.

'Who?' I said. 'Oh, it doesn't matter, if you haven't heard of "Cranky Frankie" by now, there's no point in me explaining him to you.'

'Is "Cranky' Frankie" a band?' asked Stephen.

'Stephen, go back to your computer, I'll leave his albums to you in my will – you might appreciate him by then,' I said.

Anyway, I'm sort of glad I went over and looked after the kids. It was difficult, but not in the way I thought because I got to have a talk with Tracey. I didn't bring it up, of course – the marriage business; Tracey did.

She came to me one night and said: 'Grandpa, can I talk with you for a minute?'

'Of course you can love, sit down. What is it?'

'What's going on with Mum?' said Tracey.

I froze. I sort of knew what was coming.

'Well, nothing – what makes you think there's something going on?' I said, lying through my teeth.

'Grandpa, I know there's something going on. Don't treat me like a baby, I'm fifteen!'

'What has your mum said?'

'Well, she said she was going through a difficult time and when she could talk about it, she would.'

'That's right,' I said. 'You'll have to wait until she's ready to talk about it, won't you?'

'Thanks Grandpa, that was very helpful.'

'Look Tracey, I don't know if it's my place to talk about this stuff, I'm sorry.'

'Whose place is it?' said Tracey.

Bloody kids Gene! Why do we have them? If we didn't have them, they wouldn't have children and you wouldn't have to answer a question like that.

I said, 'To be honest Tracey, I don't know whose place it is to talk to you about things like that and anyway, I'm as much in the dark about it as anyone else.'

'Mum's in love with someone else, isn't she?' said Tracey.

'Oh now, who told you that? What a lot of nonsense, your mum loves your dad.'

'Not anymore,' said Tracey.

'Don't be silly, where did you get that silly idea from?'

'Me and Stephen worked it out.'

'Did you?' I said.

'Yes.'

'Well, you're wrong! Now, what's on the telly tonight? I think *Star Wars* is on, isn't it?'

'Grandpa!' said Tracey. 'You and Nana said people should always be honest with each other.'

'No I didn't. When did I say that?'

'You've been saying that ever since we were little kids.'

'Well, that's right, but I'm not being dishonest with you Tracey.'

'What are you doing then?'

'I'm trying to avoid answering the question, that's what I'm doing.'

'So it's true.'

'Tracey, it's a bit more complicated than that, love.'

'No it isn't,' she said. 'Is mum in love with that guy Richard who used to work in the Community Centre with her?'

'No, no, no, you've got it all wrong. Look, let me explain: you see that chap, Richard, well, he thinks he's a bit in love with your mum. He's a bit fond of her. Your mum you see is...'

'In love with him,' said Tracey.

'No, she's not in love with him. She doesn't know what she wants at the moment,' I said to Tracey.

'Why didn't you just say that Grandpa?' asked Tracey.

'Well I didn't know if I should, love. Haven't your mum and dad said anything to you?'

'If I ask Mum what's wrong, she just starts crying. If I ask Dad what's going on, he says there's nothing wrong. Stephen and me had to work it out for ourselves.'

'Well, Tracey, I'm sorry love.'

'It's no big deal,' said Tracey. 'All we wanted to know was what was happening.'

'It is a big deal,' I said, 'or might be a big deal. If it turns out to be a big deal, it will be a big one, do you know what I mean?'

'Yeah,' said Tracey and she turned the television on.

'Look Tracey, if you and Stephen need to talk a bit more, it's OK to do that. It's OK to come and talk to Grandpa about it.'

'Yeah, OK,' said Tracey.

Hell, Gene, I wish you were here at the moment – I don't know what to do in situations like this. No one gives you a handbook on how to handle these things. Where's the damn road map that shows you where to go and what to say? I'll just have to play it by ear I suppose, what else can a bloke at my age do?

Anyway, enough of all this, I hope I did the right thing. Who knows? I know nothing.

I'd better choof off. Ted Davison has just finished his new shed and he's invited a few people over to celebrate. I better go; knowing Ted and his shed, we may not see him again for a while.

Hope you and your mate are OK. Write soon.

Lots of love,
Your dad

THE CARROT FESTIVAL

Kalangadoo, Monday

Dear Gene,

How are you son? You winning?

I'm doing all right. I've been busy – there was a hell of a hoo-ha in town this week. Bloody idiots down at the council are at it again.

I spent most of my time at emergency meetings of the Concerned Citizens Watch Committee. We've had enough of these dopes! We passed a resolution last night to call on the state government to get rid of them. It's unbelievable what these idiots are doing down here!

I don't know if I've told you about the galah they hired from Queensland to set up the Kalangadoo Tourist Commission. They want to try and attract the busloads of Asian tourists here on their way over to Adelaide.

Seriously, the elevator doesn't go to the top floor with some of these jokers. We thought they were pulling our leg – how can you possibly have a Tourist Commission when your town is not even on any of the bloody tourist maps?

Our Chairman, Jim Bennett, said to the Shire President, 'Why would Asian tourists want to come here? What are they going to look at?'

You know the joint, Gene. I mean we have got a couple of old buildings still standing, I suppose they're worth a bit of a look – but jeez, you're struggling to find anything remarkable after that. There are no natural attractions to speak of.

Well, there are a couple of big gum trees around the place, but cripes, no one important has ever died here. Old Bill Pearson was saying that his dad told him that a few bushrangers came through here at one time, but he couldn't remember their names and they never even stopped for lunch apparently.

I don't know. I can't see why a mob of Asians on a bus would want to come 25 miles off the main highway just to look at the post office and the Clem Miller Memorial Hall.

Still, none of this has stopped the idiots. They went ahead and hired this rattlebrain, what's his name again? The fat bugger with the suntan and the Alsatian dog – Ken Nankervis, that's it! He's flasher than a rat with a gold tooth, Nankervis!

Now what was I talking about?

Oh, that's right! So they hire Nankervis and the first thing he proclaims is that the town needs something big. Something really huge he reckoned – like the Big Pineapple in Nambour and the Big Lobster at Kingston.

Anyway they've just announced this week what we're going to get. I'm almost too embarrassed to tell you. They're going to build a Gigantic Carrot! We didn't know where to look when we heard about it!

It's going to have a spiral staircase in it and a beacon on top, and it's going to sit in the middle of the golf course and they'll use it as a fire watchtower during the summer.

Unbelievable! And if that wasn't bad enough, the stupid Mayor, Ralph Faulkner, announces that they want to turn Kalangadoo into the 'Carrot Capital of the World'. They're going to hold a bloody International Carrot Festival here next year. Talk about picked before they were ripe!

They're going to have a Miss Gigantic Carrot beauty contest, hold carrot cake bake-offs, and the local Rotary Club is going to sponsor a Bulgarian carrot expert to come over and show the locals how to grow really big carrots. They'd need to; the ones around here aren't much chop! Ted Davison's carrots, next door, are as good as anyone's, but they're nothing to write home about.

Apart from our committee, the rest of the town have gone carrot mad! People have started painting their fences orange and green. The motel has changed its name to the Big Carrot Inn and the local historical society are organising a historical re-enactment of the first carrot ever grown in Australia. I tell you, the whole town's gone nuts!

We've even got a new sign up outside the town – you know, where the Rotary and Apex welcome signs are. The sign says: 'Welcome to Kalangadoo – Home of the Gigantic Carrot'! Bloody ridiculous! People from Mount Gambier and Penola are laughing their faces off at us.

We played Penola at home at the footy on Saturday and the Penola team turned up wearing rabbit ears and eating carrots and yelling out: 'What's up, Doc?' and 'Bederp, bederp...that's all folks!'

Put our team off their game a bit, I think. It must have, we lost by 19 goals.

Talking about footy; you can't win a match sitting in the dressing room – you've got to fight the buggers – so I better get a move on. The Watch Committee is meeting over here tonight and I've run short of cheese to go with the crackers. I'll let you know how we get on.

Regards to Ahmed. Write soon.

Lots of love,
Your dad

PUSS PASSES ON &
THE FOOTY TRIP FALLOUT

Kalangadoo, Monday

Dear Gene,

How are you son?

I'm a bit upset to tell you the truth, and I'm sorry to be the bearer of bad news again. That's all I seem to do of late: write to you and tell you of the bad stuff that has happened. Someone has got to do it I suppose.

I don't know how to tell you this Gene, but it's about your sister Sharon – it's really sad. Her cat, Puss, got hit by a car yesterday and Puss is dead, gone to the big cats' home in the sky.

Sharon is beside herself as you can imagine. She's had Puss for 16 or 17 years and loved that damn cat like a child. Sharon rang me yesterday morning in tears, the poor thing, so I ended up going over there with your mother and we helped bury Puss in the backyard down by the chook house. Thought it might like a bit of company.

I think it was Puss's only regret, not getting into that bloody chook house. It fascinated her; she used to sit there for hours staring at those chooks. Of course Puss was getting on a bit and we weren't sure how long she had left anyway, but still it would have been nicer if she'd gone in her sleep I think.

The worst bit was, given the way things are between Sharon and Geoff at the moment, it was very unfortunate that Geoff was the one who ran over her. It is only going to increase the tension around there I suspect.

What happened was, Sharon and Geoff were having a blue just before it happened apparently. Geoff was running late for work, his mind was elsewhere, he just jumped into the car, didn't look and – well, I don't need to go into the details. Puss was asleep underneath the car and that's the way she stayed.

Geoff didn't even realise what he'd done. It wasn't until he got to work and Sharon rang to tell him that he'd killed her cat she'd had for 17 years.

It was an accident; it could have happened to anyone, couldn't it? Well, just about anyone. I don't know, I don't want to be unkind Gene, but you'd think if you'd run over something like a cat you would realise it, wouldn't you?

I'm not suggesting Geoff did it on purpose. Not even Sharon is suggesting that and she's probably got a few reasons to think otherwise because, let's be fair, Geoff didn't like the cat, as we all know. In fact, he hated the thing. But no one is suggesting he'd run over it, he's not that sort of person.

Of course he didn't handle the business on the phone all that well either. It didn't help things much when Geoff said to Sharon that if she was that upset, he'd pick up another cat for her on the way home. I'm not sure that was the appropriate response under the circumstances.

So anyway, that's what happened and I've got an awful feeling that this could bring a few things to a head good and proper. Geoff's already in the doghouse over the end-of-year footy trip to Adelaide the week before last.

You see, the local footy club goes on a trip to Adelaide after the season finishes and Geoff always goes. Anyway, this year someone spilt the beans about what happened on the trip and some of the wives and girlfriends are bloody furious. In fact, it's what happened on the footy trip that Sharon and Geoff were fighting over yesterday before Puss got called to her maker.

I don't know the full story of what went on, but apparently a few of the team got arrested for being drunk and brawling in the streets over there. That happens every year so no one was surprised about that, but what the wives and girlfriends were really crook on is what happened on the bus on the way down to Adelaide.

The story goes that as soon as the bus left here, they started watching pornographic movies and when the bus reaches Kingston, the footy club has hired a stripper who gets on the bus and does what a stripper does I suppose, and takes her clothes off.

No one back home would have found out about any of this, but as the bus was coming over Murray Bridge, it sideswiped a semi-trailer and the bus ended up smashing into the bridge. God knows what was going on in the bus at this stage. No one seems to know and if they do, they're not saying anything.

Then the cops turn up and start asking questions because three of the footy team and the stripper were injured and taken off to hospital in an ambulance. None of them had a lot of clothing on at the time either, according to Mrs Phipps down at the post office. Don't know how the font of all knowledge Phipps found out about it all. Probably from Beryl Coates who runs the bus station and would have milked the information from the bus driver.

Anyway, you can imagine why the wives and girlfriends are all bloody cranky. As for Geoff, he swears he had no idea they were going to show the dirty movies and that he was asleep when the stripper got on and never saw her get off. What I think he meant to say was, 'I never saw her get put in the ambulance.'

And it's not only the women who are up in arms either. Athol Pearce and the barmy Committee Against Moral Decline have come out of the woodwork and have been writing to the local paper, saying 'The recent despicable, wretched and outrageous behaviour of the Kalangadoo Magpie Football team on their trip to Adelaide is an absolute disgrace and a blot on the landscape of this community's Christian values', which it may well be, Gene.

Still, it's interesting. As Milton pointed out, Pearce's lawnmowing company is the major sponsor of the footy team and, as Milton said in his letter to the paper last week, if Pearce and his committee feel so strongly about it all, perhaps they should stop supporting the club with their sponsorship.

I said to Milton, 'Do you think Pearce will pull the sponsorship?'

'What do you reckon Roly?'

'Well, I reckon if you thought Pearce would pull the sponsorship from the footy club, you wouldn't have bothered writing the letter in the first place, would you?' I said.

'Hey, you're developing a bit of a cynical mind Roly Parks.'

'No, I'm just starting to figure out how your mind works,' I said.

Anyway Gene, what with the footy business and running over Sharon's cat, I'm afraid Geoff looks like he's 12 goals down in the last quarter and kicking into the wind. I can't see him making up the ground myself. In fact, I think the siren might go before he gets another score on the board. Either that or Sharon will take up the offer of another club, if you know what I mean.

Anyway, I better go son. Milton and I are going down to the pub to watch Ernie Watkins show a couple of Poms a thing or two about the art of dart playing.

By the way, could you send Sharon a bereavement card if you get the time. For the cat, I mean.

Give my regards to Ahmed and write soon.

Lots of love,
Your dad

THE RURAL BENEFIT

Kalangadoo, Monday

Dear Gene,

How are you son?

I'm feeling pretty good myself, but I'm run off my feet as usual. There is a big charity benefit for the drought here next weekend. My agent, Spud Turner, is running it and I'm helping out where I can.

We're going to try to organise a bit of money for the farmers. They are in a bad way over here with this bloody drought Gene; some of the farmers are so poor they're licking paint off the fence. It's terrible what's going on. People are having to sell up, leave their farms and give up what they've been doing all their lives — it's tragic.

Of course the Shire Council down here aren't lifting a finger to help the farmers either, they're too bloody mean.

Anyway, Spud is going to get a few of his artists to put a show on in Mount Gambier on Saturday night and it should be a good show the way things are shaping up.

Ricky O'Connor, the Irish comedian from Port McDonnell, is the compere, Pearl La Monde the cabaret artiste is going to do a few numbers, and they've got Rope 'Em and Brand 'Em, the big country stars, headlining the whole thing. Spud was really lucky to get them, they just happened to be performing at the cattle sales over at Border Town next week so they agreed to turn up and do a few songs. They are pretty big time nowadays; you don't get too many people along to the cattle sales unless you've got Rope 'Em and Brand 'Em on your entertainment list.

Your old mate Jimmy Lauder is going to play the didjeridu and the bagpipes – he's got to be the only joker in the world who can play both those instruments at the same time. Well, he's the only Aboriginal with a Scottish accent, I imagine, being brought up on the mission as he was.

The other big coup for the benefit was getting The Amazing Arthur, the facial illusionist act. Arthur has really hit the big time over here Gene, he was even on a breakfast TV show in Darwin a couple of months ago. He was up there doing one of those tours your mum and I used to do at the retirement homes around west Queensland and is doing really well now. It was good of him to donate his time, especially now that he's in demand.

Arthur had a bit of bad luck last week, so Spud was saying. Apparently he was set to do an audition for a spot on *The Midday Show* on Channel 9 with Derryn Hinch, but they chopped *The Midday Show* this week and Arthur missed out. It's a bloody shame – that could have made Arthur, I reckon. It would have opened up the whole RSL Club and shopping centre market for him right across the country. Still, that's show business isn't it?

Anyway, I better get my skates on, Gene. Give my regards to Ahmed and write soon.

Lots of love,
Your dad

HALF EMPTY HALF FULL

Kalangadoo, Monday

Dear Gene,

How are you son?

I'm all right, sort of. I was a bit down in the dumps about one thing or another there for a while, but I got over a few hurdles during the week so I'm feeling a bit better about myself.

Not that I was going to put the Gillette into action; it wasn't a razor blade job. It was like I was being swallowed by — well, there's no other way of putting it — swallowed by this sort of sadness. It was a bloody horrible feeling.

Anyway, thank God Milton spotted it and he's helped me sort it all out. I wonder about Milton Jones sometimes you know. I think he was given the handbook on life and the rest of us weren't. Milton can spot stuff going on in you that you don't even know is going on.

It happened one night last week. We were sitting around the fire and I was feeling really awful but kept my trap shut and tried to keep it to myself, when Milton put his book down at some stage and says to me, 'Do you want to talk about it Roly?'

'Eh, talk about what?' I said.

'Talk about what's filling up this room at the moment.'

'What are you talking about? I'm just sitting here reading the paper aren't I?' I said.

'No you're not.'

'Milton, this is a newspaper isn't it?'

'Yeah.'

'Well, I'm reading it aren't I?'

'No you're not, you haven't got your glasses on. How can you be reading anything?' he asked.

There are few things a joker can do in life, but trying to slip something past Milton Jones isn't one of them. So I put the paper that I wasn't reading down and tried to tell him about this feeling Gene, about this sadness that had come over me.

'There's a lot of sadness going around,' said Milton. 'Have you got any idea what brand name it is?'

'No idea,' I said. 'I don't know what it is really.'

'Is Sonya part of it?' asked Milton.

'Yeah, I suppose she is,' I said.

'My sister Margaret?'

'Yeah, all right,' I said.

'And your daughter Sharon's marriage?'

'Yeah, yeah it is,' I said.

'Ah, that's interesting,' he said.

'Oh, bloody fascinating Milton,' I said. 'I can't sleep without a pill, my ulcer is acting up something shocking and I'm having nightmares about holding onto people who will fall off a cliff if I let go of them. Yeah, really interesting. I'm thinking about bottling it.'

'You already have,' said Milton and then he turned and stared at the fire.

'What are you doing?' I asked.

'Oh, just thinking about all the connections in what you've said,' said Milton.

So I left him alone to think. That's what you've got to do when Milton thinks because he goes into this sort of deep, well, I don't know what it is Gene, he just goes somewhere else. He's sitting next to you but he's not with you. It's like he's gone off to the tool shed, looking for the right gadget to do the job.

Anyway, Milton kept staring into the fire and then about 20 minutes later he turns to me. 'You know what I reckon?' said Milton.

'No, what do you reckon?'

'I reckon it's more than being sad. You're grieving,' Milton said.

'Yeah, I said I was sad.'

'Yeah,' said Milton, 'but you're grieving as well. That's different from being sad.'

'What am I grieving about then?' I asked.

'Well,' said Milton, 'it's hard to say exactly. I'm only guessing, but maybe you're grieving over something you should have done but you didn't do.'

'Hang on a minute there, you've lost me son, but go on.'

'You see,' said Milton, 'I think Sharon's decision to stay with Geoff and forget this other bloke might have reminded you about what you've turned your back on. Am I right?'

'Look Milton, sometimes you don't have any choice in these matters, do you? I mean you can't just chuck your whole life up in the air because someone comes along and the rockets start firing and the legs go a bit wobbly,' I said.

'Just the same,' said Milton, 'I think you secretly wished Sharon had gone with that bloke.'

'Now what makes you think that silly bloody idea?'

'Maybe because at some stage in your life you should have gone, but you stayed. Am I right or wrong?' said Milton.

'You're bloody mad Milton!'

'I might be bloody mad, but I'm also bloody right,' Milton said, 'aren't I?'

'You're bloody mad and you're bloody right,' I said. 'Look, I've got this one voice telling me Sharon's done the right thing by staying with Geoff, and I've got another voice telling me she should have followed her heart.'

'Because you didn't with Sonya?' asked Milton.

'No – I did. But then one day whatever it was that we had wasn't there anymore, for both of us, but we stayed and we shouldn't have.'

'Yeah, I thought as much,' said Milton.

'So you reckon that's the sadness?'

'I'd stack my pension on it son,' said Milton.

'Yeah, but look Milton, I can't go telling my daughter who is semi-happily married to throw away what she's got, for what?'

'Who knows? But whatever it is, she's had a damn big whiff of it,' said Milton and then he turned his face back to the fire.

As Milton turned though, I caught this look in his eye. He sort of looked how I was feeling, just for a split second, then it was gone. 'Milton, this happened to you too, didn't it?'

'Yeah.'

'What happened?'

'Well,' said Milton, 'we walked away from it.'

'How come?'

'Well, we had to. I was free, she wasn't.'

'Ever see her again?'

'No,' said Milton, 'nor the likes of her.'

'But she's down in the shed isn't she?'

'Shed? What shed?' asked Milton.

'You know,' I said, 'the place you wander off to when you're staring into the fire.'

'Oh,' said Milton, 'yeah, down there, she's down there all right.'

'How long has she been down there?'

'Forty-two years in December.'

'Hell,' I said.

'Heaven,' said Milton. 'She was an Irish angel.'

'What was so special about her?'

'Oh, it was a lot of things,' Milton said. 'It was the way she spoke, the way she used language. She had the heart of a poet.'

'How do you mean exactly?'

'Well,' said Milton, 'I remember the day we said goodbye for the last time. We'd had a cup of tea and there were two cups, half full, with exactly the same amount in each. As Kathleen walked to the door to leave, we passed by the table and when she saw the cups, she stopped and looked down at them. Then she turned and said to me, "Tell me Milton, are the cups half empty or are they half full?"'

'What was your answer?'

'Well, I didn't have an answer,' said Milton. 'I still don't have an answer. All I know is that she wasn't talking about cups; she was talking about what we were walking away from. That's why she was special.'

'I think we better go and have a beer Milton,' I said.

So we did. We spent the rest of the night watching Ernie Watkins teaching the boys from Penola the finer points of darts.

As we were walking home from the pub I stopped Milton and said to him, 'Milton, where do you actually go when you're thinking and you go somewhere?'

'Down in the shed?'

'Yeah, down in your shed,' I said, laughing. 'Where the bloody hell is it?'

'Why?' asked Milton.

'Because I want to get another key cut so I can go there too.'

Anyway Gene, I had better scoot off. I'm meeting Sharon in town for afternoon tea and think we're going to go for a bit of a long walk.

I hope you're happy you two. Look after each other, won't you?

Lots of love,
Your dad

PARTING THE WAYS

Kalangadoo, Monday

Dear Gene,

How are you son? Are you all right?

I don't know if your mum has spoken to you yet. She said she was going to ring you with regards to Geoff and Sharon, but if she hasn't, well – Geoff and Sharon have called it quits. Well, Sharon has called it quits at least.

So it has been a really fun week around here, I'm telling you. I had your mother over here in tears most of Tuesday and Sharon's been around in tears for the rest of the week. At one stage there I had to send Milton out for tea supplies; I've never made so many pots of tea in a week.

Anyway, it's happened. Sharon and the kids are going to move in with your mum until Sharon can find a place for them all.

This probably doesn't come as much of a shock to you Gene; as you know, Sharon leaving was on the cards. I think the straw that broke the camel's back was the way Geoff behaved after he ran over Sharon's cat. It's a moral something was going to happen after that.

I can't believe I'm actually saying this to you Gene, but I really do believe it's the best thing. Sharon has given it a go for a long while now and you can't really keep going like that. If you've fired the last shot in your locker, that's it. There's no point in pretending or putting yourself through misery, is there?

Sharon was saying she would like to move to Mount Gambier to live, but the kids' school is here and she doesn't want to make it any harder on them.

I had Tracey and Stephen around here after school this week to have a bit of a chat. I think they're going to be OK. I don't know much about these things, but all they want is for their mum and dad to be happy and if that means parting the ways, the impression I got was anything that's going to stop the arguing is all right by Tracey and Stephen.

Of course they're upset and sad about it all but, as Tracey said, now they won't be the odd ones out at school. They were the only kids who were living with their original mum and dad apparently.

Geoff is turning out to be the big problem though. He doesn't want to hear about a divorce and, from what Sharon's saying, he has really strapped the martyr's cross to his back. He's saying that it's Sharon's fault and that she never really gave the marriage a shot and all that sort of nonsense.

It's silly saying things like that, Gene – I ought to know, it's what I said to your mother when we first split up. When you eventually get off your bloody high horse you realise that marriage is a bit more complicated than that. It's a *hell* of a lot more complicated than that! A damn science laboratory is less complicated than a marriage I reckon.

Anyway, Sharon suggested they go to these mediation get-togethers that your mum and I went to in Mount Gambier, but Geoff doesn't want to know about it. He reckons he'll decide when he's ready to talk about everything.

According to Sharon, she did get him to agree to attend at one stage but then he refused to go because the appointment meant he'd miss out on cricket practice. Then it was tennis practice he was going to miss, or he was busy at work.

I know what it's like Gene, it's bloody difficult. I know what your mum and I went through and at this stage of proceedings no one is listening to the other person. You say you are, but you're not really. Often you're assuming how the other person is going to react or behave, so you go and act on your assumptions instead of seriously listening to what the other person is saying. It's such a merry-go-round Gene, it happened with your mum and I a lot. Still does.

Fortunately for me, Milton picked up on it — as usual. I was talking to him about something or other one day and when I finished, he said, 'Well, have you asked Sonya what she wants?'

'Milton, I just told you what Sonya wants.'

'We know this for a fact do we?' asked Milton.

'Of course Sonya will want that!' I said.

'Yeah,' he said, 'but has she told you, or have you assumed that?'

'Milton, I'm not assuming anything. I know she will want that.'

'Roly, look, it's none of my business,' Milton said, 'and I may be wrong, but from where I'm standing, I think you're having a two-way discussion with yourself. It might be handy if you actually ask Sonya herself what she wants, don't you think?'

Well, I just looked at Milton. He was right – again. He's always right about these bloody things, Milton. There is a bloke who has got a gigantic capacity to knock you off your soapbox.

That's when I woke up to what I was doing and what your mum was doing. So I can see the problems in that area for Sharon and Geoff – especially if Geoff thinks he's got a clean bill of health and it's all Sharon's fault. He's not going to do a lot of listening to what Sharon wants under those conditions.

By the way, I rang Geoff the other day. I thought I should. I told him I was sorry about what was happening and if he wanted to drop in and have a chat any time, I was here to help. He sounded a bit like a hurt little boy, like he was the victim in the situation.

So there we go. I tell you what, maybe one week I can write to you with some good news Gene – it would make a change, wouldn't it?

Anyway, give my regards to Ahmed and write soon.

Lots of love,
Your dad

SONYA'S GARAGE SALE

Kalangadoo, Monday

Dear Gene,

How are you son?

I'm doing all right, I can't complain. Well, I could I suppose, but who listens to you? As Milton says, whingeing and complaining gets harder when you're older because you've heard yourself whinge about the same thing for so many years, your whingeing starts to get on your own nerves. He's got a point there I think. Don't know what the point is, but he's definitely got one.

It's like with your mother Gene. I mean, I know I complain about her a bit, and I don't want to, but she makes it hard sometimes.

When was it now? Saturday or Sunday, I forget, one of those days. Saturday morning — that's right, it was Milton's turn to run the messages. So, anyway, I'm sitting there, reading the paper and having a cup of tea when the phone rings. It's your mum. 'I'm having a garage sale,' she announced. 'There's a couple of things in the shed that look like they might belong to you and I thought you might like to look at them before I sell them all.'

'Too bloody right I want to look at them!'

'It's just a lot of rubbish,' said your mum.

'Well it might be a lot of rubbish to you,' I said, 'but it's my bloody rubbish. Keep your hands off it until I get over there. When is the garage sale?'

'What time is it?' asked your mum.

'It's 9 30,' I said.

'It starts in half an hour,' she said.

'Gee, thanks for the advance warning Sonya, I appreciate that.'

'Well, what did you want me to do? Tell you after I sold it all?' she said.

How can you argue with logic like that Gene? You can't, so I didn't bother.

'Why are you cleaning out the shed all of a sudden Sonya?' I asked.

'Thelma Hopgood and I are taking up pottery,' said your mum haughtily. 'We're turning the garage into a studio. Do you have a problem with that?'

'I don't care if you and Thelma are launching space rockets, just leave my stuff alone,' I said.

'It's just junk — it's been sitting around here for years. You never use any of it,' she said.

'Listen Sonya, my spare set of false teeth has been sitting around here doing nothing for years, but I don't toss them out just because I don't use them!'

'Well, you better get over here,' said your mum.

77

Anyway, I dropped what I was doing and got myself over to your mum's place quick smart. I'm not in the gate five seconds when I see this joker taking off with all my spare parts for the lawnmower. So I went up to him and said, 'Hey listen, sorry pal, but there's been a mistake. These belong to me and they are not for sale.'

'The lady just sold them to me,' said the bloke, pointing to Sonya who is approaching us at a fair rate of knots.

'Yeah, I know, but they're not hers, she had no right to sell them. I want them back.'

'Roly, the man has bought them,' said your mum in that 'I know what's good for you' voice.

'No he hasn't Sonya. He can't buy something I don't want to sell and you can't sell anything you don't own.'

'Perhaps we could discuss this inside, Roly Parks, if you don't mind,' said your mum. 'Excuse us for a minute sir, I think we can sort this out.'

'Listen, I don't want to cause a marriage break-up over lawnmower parts. If your husband doesn't want to sell them, fair enough,' he said.

'We've already broken up the marriage,' said your mum.

'Hey, Sonya, why don't you get a loud hailer? That way everyone in Adelaide and Perth can find out about our marital situation,' I said.

'Would you excuse my former husband and me just for a second?' said your mum and we went inside.

Anyway, we get inside and she says, 'Roly Parks, how dare you embarrass me like that?'

'Sonya, these are my spare parts, I bought them. What do I do if the mower packs up? Go out and buy

200 dollars' worth of spare parts that you sold for, well, whatever you sold them for. By the way, what did you sell them for?'

'I got a good price,' said your mum.

'How good?'

'Pretty good.'

'How good is pretty good?'

'Two,' said your mum.

'Too good? What do you mean too good?'

'No, you idiot,' she said. 'Two!'

'Two what?'

'Two dollars,' said your mum.

'You sold all my lawnmower parts for two bloody dollars?!'

'How am I supposed to know how much to sell them for? They're bits of junk, I wouldn't have paid a dollar for them,' she said.

'Do you know how much spare parts are for a Victor mower, Sonya?'

'No.'

'Bloody expensive,' I said.

'Hang on,' said your mother. 'They didn't have Victor written on them, it was something else, like Masport, or something.'

'Oh, Masport, are you sure?'

'Sure I'm sure,' said your mother. 'Can you use these parts on a Victor mower?'

'Oh, well it depends, doesn't it?'

'Depends on what?' said your mum.

'Well, you know, um, it depends.'

'They don't fit a Victor mower, do they Roly?'

'Look the joker's bought the damn things now Sonya. Go on, let him have them, but you're not selling anything else of mine,' I said.

Well, Gene, I never heard the end of it; your mother loves it when she scores one from me. Makes her day, makes her week and makes her life worth living, I think, your mum landing a direct hit on me.

Anyway, I better get my skates on. Give my regards to Ahmed. I hope you're both well and write soon.

Lots of love,
Your dad

GRIEVING

Kalangadoo, Monday

Dear Gene,

How are you son? You winning?

I feel like I've been through the Westinghouse washer, good and proper. Hell, what a family you belong to, Gene! Talk about irony; you're shacked up with a bloke and you are the only one who's happy!

What do I know about life? Bugger all.

It all started on Tuesday when your mother rang and said we had to talk about Sharon and Geoff and I'd better come over for tea. That was pretty ominous. Not, 'Would you like to come over for tea?' No: 'You're coming over for tea!' I should have known it wasn't going to be an easy night.

As I was walking over to your mum's down Abattoir Street, all these black cats appeared and walked across my path. Not just one cat, four of them. Talk about symbolic. Anyway, I got to your mum's house, walked in and said hello.

Your mum doesn't say a word, she just stares at me. So I said, 'Thanks for the welcoming committee, Sonya, you really shouldn't have gone to all this trouble.'

'Look, Roly Parks, I am neither in the mood for your wit or your sarcasm. Now, if you don't mind, sit down and shut up, I want to talk to you!' said your mother in that voice that freezes magpies in mid-air. So I sat down, really quickly.

'Sharon,' said your mother, 'is married to Geoff.'

'Yes, I've picked that up,' I said, trying to bring a bit of lightness into the proceedings.

'And that's how it is going to stay!' said your mum.

'Is it?' I said.

'Yes it is!' said your mum.

'How are you going to do that? What if she doesn't want to stay?'

'Sharon doesn't know what she wants at the moment.'

'I think she knows what she wants, though I'm not sure she knows what to do about it!' I said.

Anyway, this sort of back and forth goes on for an hour. So I sit there and I listen. Every time I had a point to make your mother had an answer. 'She loves Geoff,' said your mum. 'She told me!'

'Yes, I'm sure she does. I'm just not sure she's still *in* love with him!'

'So you have been putting stupid thoughts into Sharon's head!' said your mum.

'I have not!'

'You have so!'

'Look, Sonya, all I've tried to do with our daughter is to listen. It's something I learned from living with you – listening! But that's all I've done. Which is more than you've been doing, sitting up there on your moral soapbox dispensing right from wrong!'

'I beg your pardon, Roly Parks!' said your mum. 'You can leave now if you like.'

'I'm not going to leave!' I said.

'I'll ring the police!'

Well that did it for me. I'd had enough, Gene, so I got to my feet and said, 'All right, Sonya. My turn, you sit down!'

'I will not!' she said.

'*Sit down!*' I said.

Well, bugger me dead, Gene, she did.

Thank God she did, it was my last shot in the locker, I tell you. I didn't have a lot of moves left after that.

'Now, Sonya,' I said, trembling a bit. 'I've been sitting here listening to you talk at me for over an hour and I'm jack of it! The facts of the matter are, Sonya, that as I read the situation, our daughter has, unfortunately, fallen in love with another man.'

'She loves Geoff!' your mother yelled at me.

'All right, Sonya, I'm going to apologise in advance for what I'm about to say to you now.'

'What are you talking about?' said your mum.

'I've never said it to you before and I've never wanted to say it to you, so I'm really sorry but I am going to have to say it: *shut up* and for God's sake let me finish!'

Well, you should have seen the look on your mum's face! She went white, but she shut up. She actually stopped talking – for almost 15 minutes. It was a miracle, Gene. It was amazing sitting there looking at your mum's mouth and not seeing it move. It was almost beautiful, seeing the stillness of her mouth – the utter *stillness* of those lips.

So I said, 'Whether we like it or not, Sharon is in love with this bloke. I'm so sure of that now, if it was a race horse I'd be backing it! To be honest, I wish she wasn't in love with him. I wish she was still in love with Geoff because it would make everyone's life a lot bloody easier – including yours and mine.

'So the way I see it, there is no point in telling Sharon to wake up to herself. She *has* woken up to herself – that's the problem.' I finished and sat down.

At which point your mum started to cry. Then I did.

We both sat there and had a good bawl for about half an hour. More like an hour, actually. Well, we'd had a bit to bawl about together. It had been a while and we had a lot to catch up on. It wasn't just being sad, it was like Milton was saying a few weeks ago – it was grieving.

Grieving for what though? I don't know Gene. We don't have a lot of experience of it, grieving.

Grieving because you want things to stay the way they are but know deep down they can't stay the same. Letting go, I suppose, isn't it? We seem to either fight it or pretend it doesn't exist.

It's like going to a funeral. No one is allowed to really grieve at a funeral anymore. Everyone tries to hide what they really feel, to contain themselves. Make out it's not happening, that they're not really dead.

Milton reckons death is like having an elephant in your lounge room. We all know it's there but no one wants to talk about it. That's the way I think your mum and I have been carrying on. Not just about Sharon. I think what's happened to Sharon sort of brought up what's happened to your mum and me.

And it got so nasty sometimes, so damn bitter we never − well, we never buried the marriage the way it should have been buried, with full military honours. I think we have now.

I'm going to go now, Gene. I can't write anymore.

You two look after each other, won't you? What you've got is special.

Lots of love,
Your dad

A WINNER IN THE CUP

Kalangadoo, Monday

Dear Gene,

How are you son? All right?

Me? I am as happy as bloody Larry because I won the Melbourne Cup, Gene!

Well, I didn't win it personally, what I mean is that I backed a winner. It's the first time I've backed a winner since – when did Rising Fast win the Melbourne Cup now? The year he won the Mackinnon and the Caulfield.

You probably don't remember, Gene; you would have only been about four or five. 1954, that's right. That's a long time between drinks, Gene. The last two Melbourne Cups I've backed the horse that ran last – two years in a row! I reckon if you get three years in a row backing the horse that comes last, you ought to win something.

But this win was special Gene, because I actually won a bit of dough-re-mi.

I didn't win anything on Rising Fast because I couldn't get a bet on. That's the day your sister Sharon was born – I couldn't get to the pub!

After the last two Cups I wasn't even going to put a bet on. It was funny the way it all happened. Milton and I were sitting in the kitchen and Milton was studying the form guide. Suddenly he looked up from his coffee cup and said: 'Hey Roly, can you read coffee cups?'

'Can I what?' I said.

'Can you read the symbols in the coffee cups?' asked Milton.

'Nah, Sonya's sister Gwennie can, but I wouldn't have a clue. Why?' I asked.

Then Milton passed his coffee cup over to me. 'What does that look like to you?'

'It looks like some coffee grains,' I said.

'Yeah, but what shape can you make out? Does that look like a horse to you?' asked Milton.

'I suppose it does.'

'That's what I thought,' said Milton.

'So what?' I said.

'You don't think a horse appearing in your coffee cup on the morning of the Melbourne Cup is significant?' said Milton.

'Only if it's the winner and we know its name.'

'What do you reckon this bit here is?' asked Milton.

'Don't know, it looks like a stick or a post or something,' I said.

'A finishing post,' said Milton.

'It might be. What are you getting at?'

'I think this is a sign, Roly. This could be the winner of the Melbourne Cup we're looking at here,' said Milton.

'It might well be,' I said, 'but it's not much good to us if we don't know the name of the damn horse!'

So anyway, we studied the coffee grains again trying to find some idea of the horse's name. We had a look in my cup for anything that would give us a clue, but there was nothing we could make out.

'Maybe we need to have another coffee,' I suggested. 'The horse's name might show up in one of them.'

'Good idea,' said Milton.

It was a bit of a long shot Gene, of course, but the way my luck has been since 1954, picking a winner out of coffee cups was probably not as stupid as it seemed.

Anyway, we had another cup of coffee each but there were hardly any grains left in the cups. Eventually I said, 'Come on, Milton, give it away, this is stupid!'

'Don't let the Race God hear you say that Roly, you've got to keep the faith,' laughed Milton.

'Bloody Race God, I must have offended the bugger in my last life, the way he's been treating me in this one,' I said.

'No,' said Milton, 'the answer has got to be here somewhere.'

I tell you Gene, if it was anyone else carrying on like this, I would have thought they'd had kangaroos loose in the top paddock; but if Milton Jones reckons he's on to something, I've learned that there's something to be on to – if you know what I mean.

Anyway, Milton's looking around the kitchen hoping for some sort of sign that will indicate the name and after ten minutes I said, 'Come on Milton, let's go!' because we were going to go down to the pub to put a bet on anyway. I went to get my coat when I heard Milton from the kitchen: 'I've cracked it,' he yells. 'Wayne Harris!'

I hurried back to the kitchen. 'Wayne Harris? The jockey? What about him?' I said. I knew Harris had a ride in the Cup; he got in at the last minute.

'What's he riding?' asked Milton.

I looked it up in the form guide. 'Jeune, or something, an Italian name.'

'Jeune,' said Milton. 'It's French.'

'I don't know where the horse comes from,' I said.

'No, the horse's name is a French one,' said Milton. 'Well, he's going to win it. Jeune's going to win it!'

'How do you know that, Milton?'

Milton looked at me and smiled. 'What brand of coffee have we been drinking?'

I looked at the tin. 'Harris,' I said.

'That's it. Harris, Wayne Harris, the only Harris in the Cup. That's the sign. He's got to win,' said Milton.

'You're worse than my bloody sister-in-law Gwennie. Next minute you'll be having visions, Milton!'

'I told you young Harris was overdue for a win,' said Milton.

'Yeah, I know, you've been saying that for months, but...'

'Come on,' said Milton, 'let's go. I'm going to stick a couple of hundred on him.'

'You're going to what? A couple of hundred? Dollars? You're off your bloody tree Milton – you've never put more than ten bob on a horse and the tipsters here reckon it hasn't got a show. Two hundred? Milton, you need your head read!'

'I reckon I could get twenty to one from Arnie Moore,' said Milton.

Arnie Moore, Gene, is the bloke down the pub who runs a book on the sly. Don't tell anyone I told you that – Arnie will get outed by the wallopers, they'll pinch him for sure, so keep that quiet won't you?

Anyway Gene, that's what happened. I ended up sticking my neck out and put $40 on the damn horse and it won! Did very nicely, thank you very much! On top of that I decided to put $10 on an each-way bet for a place on another horse and I won that one as well. No great science there; I gave Arnie the wrong horse number by mistake and she came second. Must try that again next year – there's no point in trying to back a horse with logic is there?

We didn't do all that well at The Oaks on Thursday. We'd run out of coffee and there wasn't a jockey called 'Nescafé' in the race so we gave it a miss.

Anyway Gene, I had better choof off. Milton's shouting dinner down at the pub tonight. It should be a good night; Ernie Watkins and the boys are playing Mount Gambier at darts. I never miss Ernie when he's throwing a dart. You don't see too much genius around here, not like Ernie Watkins. So I'd better go.

Give my regards to Ahmed and tell him I think one of his mob owns Jeune, the winning horse. Sheik somebody I think owns it. I'm not sure where he's from; I don't think he's from Morocco, but he's up that way somewhere. Ahmed might even know him.

Write soon.

Lots of love,
Your dad

DOING THE BACK IN

Kalangadoo, Monday

Dear Gene,

How are you son? You winning?

Oh, I don't know if I'm Arthur or Martha at the moment!

I was sitting with Milton having a cup of tea when the phone rang. Milton answered it and turned to me and said: 'It's Sonya — and she sounds in a bad way. She's screaming in pain.'

'Oh my God,' I said, 'she's got the letter about the divorce, Milton, and she's trying to do herself in.'

'No,' said Milton, 'I don't think so. She's done something to her back. Can't move apparently.'

'Thank God for that,' I said.

'How do you mean?' asked Milton.

'Sorry, I didn't mean that. I meant thank God she hasn't tried to bump herself off or anything,' I said.

'Well, I think you better get over there.'

Anyway Gene, when I get over there, of course I can't get in. The front door is locked and your mum can't move a millimetre without her back going into spasm, so she can't open the door for me.

I can hear your mum yelling out to me but I can't pick up what she's saying, so I'm starting to get the panics. I try the windows to see if any of them are open but no luck there either.

Your mum is still yelling out at me so I think, well, I've got to do something. So I picked up a brick and smashed one of the side windows to get myself into the house. Which, as it turned out, was a bit stupid.

'Why did you smash the bloody window?' yelled your mum in pain.

'Well I had to break in, didn't I?'

'You're an idiot!' cried your mother.

Well hell, Gene, I didn't know the back door was open, did I? I didn't know that's what your mother was going on and yelling about. A joker makes mistakes under pressure.

Anyway, that was only half of it, Gene. As I bend down to see if your mum still has feeling in her back, my back went. The pain, Gene, was excruciating. I'd ripped a muscle just like your mum had. I still can't believe it!

Sometimes, Gene, I think to myself when these things happen that I must have offended the God of Chaos or something in my last life. I'm starting to think your sister Sharon is right about all that stuff. I know I've offended the Goddess of Cars in my last life, no doubt about that. It's the only way to explain why my car never works properly. Same with my life.

Really, Gene, I don't mind having a bit of bad luck, fair enough. God's got a right to spread bad luck around a bit, we should all have our share, but I think God's got his roster system mixed up and I'm copping someone else's bad luck on top of my own.

So anyway, there we are, your mum and me, the two of us lying on the lounge room floor writhing in pain. Talk about a bad scene in a movie; if it hadn't been so bloody painful, you'd have laughed your head off, which is what Sharon had to stop herself from doing when she arrived ten minutes later with old Doc Wilson in tow.

She didn't know I was there, let alone that I was lying on the floor next to your mother, the both of us looking like – well, looking like we might have on our wedding night. You know what I'm saying Gene.

'God almighty!' said Sharon. 'What have you two been doing?'

'Just get some bloody Bex tablets,' I yelled, every word making my back feel like it had a knife in it.

As for bloody old Doc Wilson, misery guts there, did he offer any sympathy? No, you'd get more sympathy from a serial killer than that old basket case.

'Now,' said Doc Wilson in that patronising tone of his, 'how did we get ourselves into all this?'

Oh, I thought, I'd love to say, 'This is embarrassing, doctor. The wife and I were having wild sex in front of the telly and we didn't know when enough was enough.' I was going to say that Gene. Through the pain I had this little voice in my head saying, 'Go on Roly, make the bugger blush', but I didn't. I was in enough trouble with your mum over the broken window.

So anyway, I explained the story. 'Well now, you'll both need to stay in bed for at least four or five days. Can someone help you, or should we book you both into the hospital?'

'Like hell!' I said.

'No, thank you very much Doctor Wilson,' said your mum.

So anyway, they organised an ambulance to get me home, and Sharon and Milton have been running a shuttle service with food to your mum's and back ever since.

And thank God I remembered the letter I sent to your mum about the divorce, Gene. I mean, can you imagine? I got Sharon to pick up the mail and I told her to hang onto it until your mum gets better.

Anyway, I'm getting a bit tired talking about this, Gene, I'd better scoot. Give my regards to your mate and write soon.

Lots of love,
Your dad

VALE THE DUNNY RUN

Kalangadoo, Monday

Dear Gene,

How are you son? You winning?

I should tell you Gene, a bit of history has just ended here this week. Old Bomber Balnaves' dunny run has been finally closed down by the council.

They've been threatening to close it down for years but there were too many thunderboxes still around the joint, so they backed off. Well, there was only Ruby Cunningham's left but they finally convinced her to go a bit modern and give it up.

Have to give it to Ruby, she went down fighting, Gene. Threatened to take the council to court over it. The council were reluctant for years because any time they take Ruby on, she gets her gander up. She's like a mad dog and won't let go.

I think the council remembered the last time they took her on — when they replaced the stop signs with roundabouts and Snowy Thompson's semi with a hundred head of cattle hit the roundabout and careered into her bedroom. Ruby sued the council for attempted murder and they settled out of court.

Anyway, they finally convinced Ruby to give up the thunderbox. Struck a pretty good deal still, old Rube – council have had to fork out to put in all the sewerage and the new toilet. Renovated part of the farmhouse to accommodate it all.

Funny, I remember many years ago when your mum and I got our first loo – you were just a young tacker. I was against the idea of having an inside loo at first. Well, I didn't know what was what. The thought of having a thunderbox inside the house didn't appeal to me much.

I couldn't see how dragging all that sawdust into the house was an advancement, you know what I mean? Then they pointed out it was a cistern type of arrangement. You know, it was all sort of automatic. You pressed a button and everything just disappeared. You didn't need to throw sawdust down it either.

Still, the writing was on the wall for Bomber's night cart business once the indoor loo took off. His son, Bill, was supposed to take over the business at one stage but I think young Bill saw what was coming and went into the retail side of the business: selling loos. It's been a big part of our history though, the night cart. It's been coming and going for over 100 years.

Speaking of cutting things – bloody local council! They get on my quince the way they've been carrying on lately, cutting this, cutting that. They've even cut out the cutting!

They've cut out the Cemetery Grass Cutting Grant to the Lions Club and no one can get at their dead anymore.

You should see the cemetery – what am I saying? You can't see it, that's the problem. It's all covered in couch grass!

Thelma Hopgood was telling me she tried to get up there the other week. She got halfway up the hill, heard a rustle in the grass, turned around and there's this bloody great tiger snake staring at her. She was off like a bride's nightie she reckoned!

Something is a bit crook when a woman can't put flowers on her husband's grave; it's criminal – the place is going to the pack.

The council sold the local tip to a developer from Queensland and do you know what the galah's gone and done? Stuck a bloody housing estate on it. On the tip!

It's called 'The Bonza Life Housing Estate' and has got all these expensive houses and man-made lakes and canals on it. The local papers described it as 'The Venice of the South East'. Well, they got the Venice bit right – the bloody thing is sinking a foot a month.

And where they stuck the international golf course, the chemicals from the tip underneath have started eating into the greens. It's dreadful, there's rubbish coming up from everywhere through the sand traps – it's a shocker. No one can play on the damn thing because honestly, the smell would make a blowfly sick.

Here's the best bit: the developer shot through a week or so ago – to Spain, apparently.

Doesn't surprise me the whole thing came off the rails. I mean, if you stick a housing estate on top of a local tip, on top of an Aboriginal sacred site, it's a moral something is going to happen. Bad karma, your sister Sharon said. Very bad karma, I reckon – *extremely* bad karma.

Anyway, better be on my way. Give my regards to Ahmed — I hope his ballet business is going OK — and write soon.

Lots of love,
Your dad

THE MERRY-GO-ROUND

Kalangadoo, Monday

Dear Gene,

How are you son? All right?

I'm not bad myself, considering, but hell, it's been a busy week. I thought things were going to ease up a bit, but they haven't. Well, I thought things were going to ease up six months ago, but I don't think there's any such thing as a quiet week anymore.

There used to be quiet weeks when a joker could sit around, do nothing and get a bit bored with himself. It's nice being bored occasionally, but you can't do it anymore.

It's not just me Gene, everyone's bloody busy: busy doing this, busy doing that and if it's not that, it's this, or this and that. Even when you're chatting to people on the phone, they don't tell you they're busy. They don't have to; you can hear it in their voice. Gone are the days when you could sit on the phone and have a chinwag with someone.

Anyway, I'll stop moaning. What have I been up to? What's been going on?

Well, your sister Sharon was over for tea during the week and she's doing all right under the circumstances. The problem is Geoff is still acting like a bit of a galah.

He keeps ringing Sharon every day at work – not once either, but three or four times a day. Then he's on the phone to her four or five times at night at your mum's place, saying he wants her to come back and that he can't live without her and he'll do whatever it is she wants him to do, as long as she comes back home.

I think Geoff's a bit weak in the head, Gene, that's no way for a grown-up to carry on. It's a bit late in the day to say you'll change; the horse has bolted – especially in Sharon's case.

You can't change just like that, can you? You can change your habits, but you can't change your personality. That's Geoff's problem; he doesn't have a personality. I mean, he's got a personality of course – we all have one – it's just that the personality Geoff's got isn't the one Sharon is interested in anymore.

Anyway, the phone calls are really getting on Sharon's quince. I said to her, 'What do you talk about with him?'

'We talk about the same stuff we went over 50 times the last time he phoned,' said Sharon. 'It just goes around in circles. Geoff says I've got to come back home and I say to him I don't have to do anything and Geoff asks, "So this is really it, is it? I mean it's really it? It's really over, that's what you're saying?" and I say, "Yes, it is really over, how many times do I need to tell you this before it sinks in?"'

'Then Geoff hangs up on me and I sit and wait for the phone to ring again because I know he'll call back and apologise and off we'll go again. Eventually he will start accusing me of things, so I'll hang up and so it goes on, Dad. It's a bloody merry-go-round.'

It happened every night last week apparently. It would drive me bonkers. I don't know how long you put up with that sort of thing. Your mum answered the phone the other night when he rang because Sharon didn't want to speak to him; she'd had enough of it. Anyway, your mum told Geoff that Sharon was out and when Geoff asked where she was, your mum said, 'Look, I'm not my daughter's secretary, I don't know where she is.'

When Geoff told Sonya that he thought she *did* know but wasn't telling him, your mum said that it was Sharon's business where she went. That's when Geoff and your mum had a big blue apparently. Sharon said she'd never heard your mum go wild like that. Crikey, you'd want the film rights to an event like that. What really got up Sonya's gander was when Geoff accused your mum and me of breaking up their marriage.

I said to Sharon, 'God, he didn't say that, did he? What colour did your mum turn when he said that to her?'

'White, then sort of bluish, then very purple,' said Sharon.

Obviously, Geoff had been drinking, Gene. He didn't know what he was taking on. It's either a very brave man or a bloody idiot who accuses Sonya Parks of anything – let alone pointing the bone at her for breaking up her daughter's marriage.

I said to Sharon, 'It's a wonder your mum didn't reach down the telephone line and grab Geoff's throat.' He must have been drinking, Gene, he must have been.

Good thing he didn't say it to me either, I would have sorted him out good and proper. Still, not as good as your mother is going to sort him out in the future. Hooley dooley, talk about a joker not valuing his life. If I were Geoff, I'd be thinking about buying a watchdog and putting landmines around the house.

After Sharon told me all this the other night, I thought about it and ended up ringing Geoff's mum, Peg. Peg and I are still mates and I thought she might be able to talk to Geoff. I told Peg what had happened and Peg had tried to talk to Geoff but he wouldn't listen to her either.

In the end, Peg had told Geoff to stop acting like an eight-year-old and that he ought to grow up and stop feeling sorry for himself. Now Geoff doesn't speak to his mother anymore. It's going to be a pretty short Christmas card list for Geoff this year if he keeps up this sort of behaviour.

Speaking of Christmas, it looks like it's going to be a real bucket of laughs around here the way things are going at the moment. You wouldn't happen to have a spare bed for an old digger in London at Christmas, would you Gene? I'm thinking of packing my swag and getting out of here.

I'm serious, I'm thinking of ringing Margaret and Milton and seeing if they might like a white Christmas this year. It's going to be pretty red around here from the blood being spilt.

Anyway, I had better go. I've got to do a bit of shopping for tea. Give my regards to Ahmed – I hope you're both well. Write soon.

Lots of love,
Your dad

MRS ELIZA CURTIS SCOTT JONES

Kalangadoo, Monday

Dear Gene,

How are you son? You winning?

What's been happening this end? A wedding!

My agent, Spud Turner, rang me last week in a bit of a panic. He had booked this joker to MC a wedding in Mount Gambier, but the intended MC got so fed up with the bride's mother-in-law sticking in her two bob's worth about the wedding reception, he chucked in the towel.

So Spud rang me and asked me to fill in as MC, conveniently omitting any mention of the mother-in-law or why the original MC spat the dummy, but after an hour with the mother-in-law from hell, I wanted to spit the dummy myself, Gene. But now I can't. I'll tell you why – it was a real turn up for the books!

Well, I front up to the client's house to talk about the reception and the mother-in-law has got the big house, the face lift and has had a complete politeness bypass. You know the type who comes into money; they marry a rich bloke, he falls off the perch and she lives the life of Reilly.

Trouble is they haven't learnt any manners. Or if they had manners, they lost them when they got married into money.

It was two days before the wedding. I was ushered in and before I've had the chance to sit down she said, 'What are your credentials for the job?'

I looked at her and said, 'My name is Roly Parks and I'm not here for an audition.'

'Well, one would like to feel confident that you can do the job,' she snapped.

'Well, one wouldn't be here if one didn't think one could do the job. Listen, Mrs whatever-your-name-is, we haven't been introduced.'

'Mrs Eliza Curtis Scott Jones.'

'How do you do?' I said.

We sat down with the happy couple and started talking about the reception. Her son was too scared to say 'boo' and whenever the bride uttered a peep, Mrs Eliza Curtis Scott Jones sticks her bib in and dismisses everything the poor girl had to say.

After an hour of this, the woman was giving me a roaring headache and the poor groom and bride-to-be left the room in tears threatening to call the wedding off. That did it for me, so I said 'Look, I'm not sure I'm the right bloke for this role.'

'What's the problem?' demanded Lady Muck of the Fowl-house.

'Well, to be honest, what you want seems to be at odds with what everyone else wants.'

'I'm paying for it!' she shrilled.

'Yes, but it's their wedding. You are going to turn their day into a misery, if you ask me. I've been here for two hours, we're not getting anywhere, and to be frank, I'm getting a bit jacked off with your manner.'

'How dare you speak to me like that? You can leave now if you wish,' she said.

'Fine,' I said, 'no skin off my teeth.'

So I got up and left. Within an hour I got a call from her. 'Mr Marks?'

'Parks.'

'Mr Parks, look, one has been under *immense* pressure and perhaps I've been a little demanding. I apologise. Would you reconsider?'

I said I would; however, I'd need to have a private discussion with her before I finally agreed.

Now, here's the funny thing Gene. From the moment I'd met her I kept thinking that I knew her face from somewhere and the name Curtis rang a bell.

I was so sure, when I got home I rang my old mate Bluey Dawson in Adelaide. 'Bluey, does the name Curtis mean anything to you?'

'Curtis?' He thought for a while and then said, 'Well, back in the early days there was a Nancy Curtis who was a dancer from the Tivoli. Do you remember her?'

That's when the penny finally dropped. Of course! That's who Eliza reminded me of – Nancy Curtis!

'Did she have a daughter?' I asked.

'Yeah, she had a daughter who eventually married some rich bloke. From memory her name was Elizabeth or Eliza, something like that.'

Nancy Curtis's daughter, that's who she was!

Nancy is long dead now, but she was a beautiful woman with a heart of gold. The problem was that she had married an absolute tosser, got in the grip of the grape and ended up running everything from two-up games to SP booking houses of ill repute. No wonder young Eliza reinvented herself.

Anyway, yesterday I went round to have a word with Eliza. I sat down and said to her, 'Before I agree to do this MC business, I need to tell you that I knew your mum, Nancy Curtis. She was a dancer at the Tivoli theatre.'

Well she nearly died, Gene. She went to protest and I cut her off. I said, 'Eliza, I know you and your mum had a pretty tough life and I don't want to blow your cover here, so I'll make you a deal. You stop being a pain in the rear-end to everyone and let your son and his bride work this reception out, or at the wedding I swear I'll give them a speech they'll be talking about round here for years!'

Well, Eliza looked at me and then said, 'Mr Parks, can I offer you a Scotch? I think we need one.' We then spent the next three hours talking about her mum, Nancy.

You wouldn't be dead for quids, Gene, would you? Anyway, I had better go. Love to Ahmed. Write soon.

Lots of love,
Your dad

SPRUNG IN MILLICENT

Kalangadoo, Monday

Dear Gene,

How are you son?

Thanks for your letter, it was nice to hear from you. Congratulations on your new job – Artist Liaison Officer with the Royal Ballet – that's great news! I imagine you'll meet a lot of interesting types of people, half your luck!

Anyway, I need to let you in on what's happened here last week. She's on for young and old around this neck of the woods, Gene. I'm in the poop good and proper!

And what did I do? Nothing! All I did was go out to dinner in Millicent with Milton's sister, Margaret, who was over from Melbourne.

The only reason we ventured out on our own was because Milton was crook. He wasn't feeling a hundred so we just went. And what did we do? It was hardly a heinous crime, Gene; we had an Indian meal at the Maharajah of Millicent and came back to Milton's and watched the telly.

It's not as if Margaret and I were smooching or making whoopee together. I never went near the woman. I gave her a peck on the cheek before she went to bed but I'd do that saying goodnight to Thelma Hopgood or Marge Johnston – it doesn't mean I've got eyes for them.

Obviously one of Beryl Coates's vigilantes must have spotted us in Millicent and started sending morse code messages or smoke signals back to Gossip HQ. Your mum would have got a call from Mrs Phipps from the post office; bloody Phipps would have told your Auntie Gwennie and that would have guaranteed the whole town would know about it within an hour.

The whole thing has been a bloody nightmare. Your mother reckons she won't have anything to do with me again. In fact, she rings me three times a day to tell me this. She says I ought to be ashamed of myself, that I'm an adulterer and that I ought to learn to keep me fly done up. On top of that she refers to Margaret as 'that brazen hussie' and she's started calling me Errol Flynn.

I think I'll end up in the giggle factory if this keeps up. Can you certify yourself? Think I might have to.

I've tried to explain to your mother that nothing was going on, but it doesn't sink in. I lost my block at her this morning when she rang. I said, 'Look, Sonya – what's it to you what I do anymore?'

'What do you mean?' she demanded.

'For God's sake! You say you don't want me back in a fit.'

'No I don't!' she said.

'Well, there you go,' I said.

'What's your point?' she says.

'My point is on the one hand you want to throw me overboard and yet as soon as you think I've tipped my hat at another woman, you stack on a turn! What am I supposed to do – be like the bloody Flying Dutchman, floating around forever on my own?'

'So you were out canoodling with "Lana Turner" – I knew it! You're just a dirty old man,' she snaps and hangs up.

The worse part about it is, as I said, the whole town knows about it. I saw Soapy Butler and his wife down at the pub the other night. I knew they knew about it, because Soapy offered to buy me a drink. I knew something was up if Soapy Butler's offering to buy me a drink; he wouldn't shout if a shark bit him, Soapy Butler. The man's still got his lunch money from school.

I kept my trap shut because once Soapy's wife gets onto a story, you're likely to hear about it internationally.

Anyway, I better hit the bitumen. I've got the marriage counsellor's appointment in an hour and I've got to find some protective headgear to wear given what your mother's going to throw at me. Say your prayers for me.

Give my regards to Ahmed and write soon.

Lots of love,
Your dad

STUCK IN THE PAST

Kalangadoo, Monday

Dear Gene,

How are you son? You winning?

Look, I'm sorry I haven't written but I've been in Adelaide for Meryl and Burt Reed's golden anniversary. You remember Meryl and Burt Reed, don't you?

Funny thing happened too. Guess who else was over there? Milton's sister Margaret happened to be going over to Adelaide for a wedding at the same time. Talk about a coincidence!

Anyway, I stayed at your uncle Lance's place for a night – just the one night. One night at Lance's is enough. I mean, one night there is like a month anywhere else. Honestly, I don't know how your poor aunty Kay has put up with Lance over the years, Gene; she is more like his mother than his wife.

It's true, I've been saying it for years: I don't know why she stuck it out. Your aunty Kay could have married anyone – she's a lovely woman, smart, clever, funny as buggery and a beautiful-looking woman even now. She reminds me of Katharine Hepburn. Why she married your uncle Lance has still got me beat.

I remember saying to her once, 'Kay, what on earth possessed you to marry my brother?'

'Because he asked me,' she said.

'Yeah, but a lot of jokers must have asked you that question over the years.'

'Yes they did,' she said.

'Well, why did you choose Lance of all people?'

'Because no one could sing "Danny Boy" like your brother could – then or now,' she said.

I don't know, Gene, who knows the mind of a Catholic girl? Not me, I think I'll go to my grave being baffled by them.

So I stayed with Kay and Lance for the night and we did what we always do when I go over; we sit around the fire and talk about the old days. It's the same stuff we always talk about, telling the same old stories we've told a thousand bloody times before, and then out comes the beer and the Irish songs and Lance eventually falls asleep – or we do. Mission accomplished.

It was strange this time Gene. None of this used to bother me before because that's just what you did when you went over there and saw your family. I never took much notice of it but this time around just going back over the same old ground all the time, it really got on my quince. Especially when I tried to talk about anything that was going on in my life now with Sharon and your mum and all that.

It was like they didn't want to know what was going on with me now. They just wanted to talk about the past

– what used to go on. It's like they don't want to know that you've changed. I think it scares them or something.

I tried to talk to Lance and Kay about a few things but as soon as I did, Lance headed to the fridge for a Guinness and started singing 'I'll take you home again Kathleen' and Kay pulled out her knitting. I felt like a stranger. It's a terrible thing to admit to, Gene, but I was glad to go.

Then I got over to Meryl and Burt's and it was the same damn thing over at their place. It was lovely to see them of course, but as soon as I mentioned anything past 1948, their eyes seemed to glaze over and Meryl would get up and make a pot of tea and Burt would switch the telly on.

I wouldn't have dared to tell them about Margaret and me, or that she was in town – good heavens! And Gene, I'm talking about two of my oldest friends. I thought to myself, I can't talk to these people anymore. I've known them half my life and I couldn't talk to them. The sad thing is Gene, I don't think I'll ever be able to talk to them about this stuff again.

Maybe Sharon is right; you can still love someone, but sometimes you just grow apart. No one is to blame, it just happens.

As you can imagine, I was really glad that Margaret was over there – as I said, what a coincidence that was! And for God's sake, don't tell this to anyone, but after a night at Meryl and Burt's, I didn't want to stay anymore, so do you know what I did? I took off! I told them a mate of mine was crook and I was going to go and stay with him and I galloped away.

I can't believe I did it, but I did. I booked into the same hotel as Margaret. Not with her, not in her room, I had my own quarters – everything was above board – but I stayed at the hotel for the rest of the time.

What happened was that Margaret had gone off to her friend's wedding reception that night and I went off to Meryl and Burt's golden anniversary at the RSL Club. It only got worse when I got there, Gene. I ran into all these people I hadn't seen for years and all they wanted to talk about was the good old days. What 'good old days'? They weren't good old days! God it was boring! I felt like I was suffocating.

Don't get me wrong. These are nice people and it's not that I think I'm better than they are Gene, I don't – no way, it's not that. But they were like the walking dead. That's a horrible thing to say, isn't it? A man of my age talking like that, but it's true; you could actually see it in their eyes, like they'd given up. The bodies are still alive but it's like the soul has called it quits – like the spark plugs have given up.

Some of these people are in their early seventies and life has just become a routine, like Mum and Dad's old vaudevillian show. They'd come out every night, do the same dance routine, tell the same bad old jokes and hate what they were doing, but they'd never changed anything – too frightened. By the time they got the courage up to do something new, the audience were chucking vegetables at them.

What is it? I don't know. Fear I suppose. It's a funny thing, fear; fear of what people will think and of what they might do if you tell them something new. You could live your whole bloody life like that.

That's why I like Margaret and Milton, because they're not frightened of all those things. I think their attitude might be rubbing off on me a bit.

Anyway, Margaret and I arranged to meet after she'd been to the wedding and I'd been to Burt and Meryl's and I couldn't wait to get out of there. I was supposed to meet Margaret at 10 pm at the hotel for a drink, but by 8.30 that evening I just wanted to take off. So I rang the wedding reception venue and got Margaret on the phone. I asked her how she was going and she said she was trying to stay awake. So I said, 'Haven't you got a bad headache?' Margaret said she hadn't, but could develop one pretty quickly and asked what I had in mind. I replied anything but a golden anniversary dinner at an RSL club. So we both fled and met up at the hotel half an hour later.

I've never done anything like that in my life Gene. I have wanted to plenty of times, but I've never been brave enough to do it. It's shocking, isn't it? I mean, really, a joker my age behaving like that and, while I feel as guilty as hell Gene, I don't regret it.

Anyhow, Margaret and I spent a couple of lovely days wandering around the place and then I had to come back to Kalangadoo. By another happy coincidence, Margaret was coming to see her brother Milton, so she came back on the bus with me.

That was last week. I don't know when Margaret is heading back, I think next week sometime.

Anyway Gene, I had better go. I'm cooking dinner tonight for everyone at Milton's. We're having Malaysian something or other. I've never cooked it before but if it turns out as good as the Mexican number I whipped up the night before last, I'll be as happy as Larry.

It's nice being happy, isn't it? I hope you and your mate are. Give my regards to Ahmed, won't you?

Lots of love,
Your dad

DRAIN STOPS THE PLAY

Kalangadoo, Monday

Dear Gene,

How are you son?

I'm all right. Just. Been under sustained attack from your mother's northern flank but I've finally found a way to halt the panzer attack.

The last few weeks I got really fed up with defending myself all the time at these marriage counsellor get-togethers. Your mother's been bowling googlies at me for seven months now and I've never been able to work out which way she was going to turn the ball, and I'd just had enough. Wasn't getting anywhere.

Anyway, I was chatting about all this to Milton Jones and Milton said to me: 'Roly, life's only difficult for a batsman if he plays the spinners off the back foot. Keep doing that and you are going to get out eventually. What you've got to do every now and then is move your feet, hop down the wicket and lift a few over the bowler's head. That sorts them out,' he said.

I thought Milton, you're a cracker! That's what I've been doing wrong; playing life on the back foot. Well, no more: enough, I thought. At my age I haven't got a lot left in the innings so it's time to hit a few to the boundary before I pull up stumps.

So in I went to the counselling session and before your mum could start the day's play, I pounced. I said hello to your mum and Raelene the counsellor and then I said, 'Before we kick off, I'd like to say a few things, if I may?'

Well, your mum glared at me with that 'Don't you try and worm your way out of this, Roly Parks' look.

I said, 'I've been coming here for seven months listening to the case against me. Now I'm not saying there isn't a case to answer; I can't have logged up all these complaints without there being some truth in it – I accept that. I've let Sonya here have her say, but I realise now that she's going to keep having her say until I get up and insist on mine, and today I'm going to have *my* say!'

Or words to that effect. I was pretty nervous.

Anyway, that's when it happened, Gene. Instead of saying I just wanted to have my say, I said 'Sonya, I'm sorry I've made your life bloody miserable. I am *really* sorry. It's pretty clear that I've got a black dog on me and I can't see how I'm going to get rid of the mongrel just sitting around here week after week while you use me for target practice.'

Your mother had gone white at this stage and if looks could kill, I would have been six foot under pushing up geraniums. Then I just kept going. Surprised the hell out of myself.

'So, what I'm saying is, what is done is done and it's pretty obvious to me it can't be undone, so I think I want to finish the match. I want to take my bat and go home.'

'Yes, and do what?' asks the counsellor.

'I don't know – practise up against a brick wall somewhere on my own!' I said.

Well, you could have heard a pin drop. Your mum just looked at me with her mouth open.

'Well, if that's how you feel,' says your mum.

'That's how I feel.'

'So, this is it?' your mum asks.

'Yes, whatever it is – this is it!' I said.

Then I just got up and walked through the door, just like that. Game abandoned.

So there you have it Gene. I'm not going back. Whatever happens from here on in, I'll just have to accept it.

Sorry to burden you with all this. I'd better go. I think I need a Scotch.

Lots of love,
Your dad

TWO TRAINS RUNNING

Kalangadoo, Monday

Dear Gene,

How are you son? You all right?

I'm sorry I haven't written for a while son, but to be honest I haven't had much to tell you.

I don't want to keep boring you to death with the family carry-on all the time, I'm sure you've heard enough of it all. Life is like a bad soap opera around here at the moment. I don't know if you're jack of it all, but I am. I'm bored with it Gene, fed up to the gills.

On top of that, Milton has been away for a week, so I'm really bored with myself. In fact I'm so bored, I've watched television for two nights in a row. It's a sure sign you're bored when you need the idiot box to keep you company. You know what it's like here in town, Gene: on the Richter scale of excitement, the needle doesn't register above zero most of the time – except during the Carrot Festival.

Maybe I need to move somewhere else, perhaps to Mount Gambier. Not that Mount Gambier is on the jetsetters' preferred destination list, but at least things other than the pub are open after nine o'clock at night.

I miss Milton when he takes off. Thank God I moved in with him; I think I'd end up at the funny farm if I didn't have Milton to talk to. Milton's got these sort of anti-boredom devices built into him or something.

Being on your own you have all this time on your hands and you don't know how to use it. The worst thing is when you've got a bit of time on your hands, you look around and realise how boring bits of your life really are. It's a bloody worry when you do that. You've got to keep busy otherwise you start sitting around eyeing your navel too often and you go crackers. Little men in white jackets come along and get you in the middle of the night if you do that for too long.

I mean, there are friends you can pop in and see and have a natter to, but you can't be doing that all the time, can you? What are you going to talk about – what you talked about the day before? They'd get sick of you. 'Oh quick, shut the curtains Myrtle, bloody Roly's here for a chat again.'

Your friends tell you they don't say things like that and they probably don't, but you feel like they're feeling like that. I didn't explain that very well.

I was talking to Milton about this the other day before he went away. He lived by himself for a long time after his wife passed on. I said, 'Milton, do you know that feeling that you get when you can't get out of your own way and nothing you do seems to satisfy you? It's like there's something missing. It's been giving me the bloody willies lately. What is it?'

'The thing that's missing?' asked Milton.

'Yeah, you know when you get bored with everything? With life?'

Well, Milton just gave me one of those looks he gives you when he's about to tell you something.

'Look, Roly,' he said, 'it's not hard to work out. I mean, you spent most of your life, like I did, with a partner – you're just missing being intimate with someone.'

'Sex?' I said. 'Do you reckon I'm bored because I need to have sex? You're mad, Milton!'

'I didn't say sex,' said Milton. 'You can be intimate with someone without having sex.'

'Sure,' I said, 'you're preaching to the converted on that one Milton. So what are you trying to say to me – that I need a partner?'

'Well, you want the closeness you get that you can't get with anyone else,' he said. 'You know what it's like when you're really close, it's like you are two trains running together on parallel lines.'

'I know what you mean. Sonya and I were like that once.'

'When was that?' said Milton.

'1953. I can't remember much after that though. No, I'm just joking around Milton, but it has been a long time between drinks,' I said.

'No it hasn't,' said Milton. 'I've seen you running along the railway lines together with someone.'

'Running along the railway lines with whom? When?' I said.

'My sister, Margaret,' said Milton.

'Get out of here Milton, what are you going on about? Look, Margaret and I are not on any, what is it we were supposed to be running on again?'

'Parallel tracks,' said Milton.

'No, it doesn't seem like that to me.'

'Well, where are you?' said Milton.

'I don't know, in a holding pattern at 30,000 bloody feet the way things are at the moment.'

'Yeah,' said Milton, 'but that will change. But if I'm right, if Margaret was around here, you wouldn't be having this conversation with me, would you?'

'Yeah, all right smarty pants,' I said. 'Well, what about you? I mean, you're on your own – whose running along the railway lines with you at the moment? Have you got a train you're fond of?' I asked.

Milton didn't say anything, he just smiled. I thought, you sneaky bugger. 'You have, haven't you Milton? Who is it? How long has this been going on?'

'Well, we're still in the station. I don't know where we're going – it might not be anywhere, but I'll let you know if we get up a bit of steam,' Milton said, laughing.

He's a worry, Milton Jones. No wonder no one in town asks him to play at their card games; talk about play your cards close to your chest. Milton is the original Cool Hand Luke.

Anyway, how did I get on to all this again? I didn't mean to. Give my regards to your mate, I hope you're both happy and on the same railway track. Write soon.

Lots of love,
Your dad

IN THE POOP

Kalangadoo, Monday

Dear Gene,

How are you son?

I'm all right, sort of. By that I mean I'm still alive by the skin of my teeth. I suppose your mother's rung and you probably already know I'm in the poop with her in a big way. I got sprung, Gene; your mum found out that I went to Melbourne and stayed with Milton's sister, Margaret.

Talk about your mother milking it for everything it's worth, talk about drama Gene, you haven't seen anything like it. It's like the last scene from *Macbeth* down this way; your mother has really spat the dummy this time. She has already spoken to Orrie Carmichael, the solicitor, to find out how she goes about getting the divorce, which, given we've been separated for so long and we've given up the ghost, is probably overdue anyway.

What I want to know is how she found out; I'm buggered if I know how she did. I know you and Sharon didn't tell her because I asked you not to. I double-checked down at the bus station to make sure there was no one around there that knew your mother or me. It's got me beat who dobbed me in.

Someone must have seen me get on the bloody bus. Damned place, there are too many people around here with nothing better to do than dob you in. She's got spies everywhere, your mother, a bloody network of them. You can't do anything. I mean, your mother hears about everything I do before I do it.

I was talking to Jack Hennessy about it the other day at the pub and he reckons there's a group of them called 'The Grapevine' and they have meetings and swap information about the men in town and what they're up to, who they're drinking with at the pub and that sort of thing. Well, I don't know about that. I mean, Jack hasn't been that well since his wife ran off with the other woman in the sixties.

Still, it wouldn't surprise me, but it'll be a moral to be one of the Op Shop Vigilantes.

I can't figure it out. Hang on a tick, hold your horses… *Beryl Coates*, she runs the bus station down there. No, she wasn't on duty that day, I checked that. Wait a minute, she runs the place so would have seen the list of the names of people getting on the buses. She'd have taken a peek, couldn't help herself.

I think I'm on to it Gene. Of *course* it was Beryl Coates, she doesn't miss a trick.

You can't go anywhere in town without seeing Beryl Coates snooping around the place. You go down the shop, she's there. You go down to Mount Gambier to have a few drinks with a few mates and who is sitting in the lounge room? Secret Agent Coates!

I think they've cloned that woman, you know. She's like Superman the way she can get from one place to another so quick; nobody can be in so many places at one time. Yeah, I think I've solved it. No doubt about it – Secret Agent Coates, guilty as charged, Your Honour.

Speaking of guilt, I rang your mother when I got back because I knew something was up. You know how you get that feeling in your bones when something bad is about to happen to you? Well I got a dirty big feeling just as I picked up the phone.

'G'day Sonya,' I said, trying to pretend everything was Jake. 'How have you been?'

Silence. Not just any silence, Gene: graveyard silence. I knew then that I was a gonner.

'Sonya,' I said, 'it's Roly.'

'Roly? Roly who?'

'Sonya, it's Roly!'

'Roly Parks?' she said.

'I just rang up to see how you were getting on Sonya.' Silence. 'Sonya, how are you getting on?'

'Is this Roly Parks the liar, or is it Roly Parks the dirty old man who can't keep his zip done up?'

Oh dear God, I thought. Beam me up Scotty, life as I know it is coming to an end.

'What are you talking about Sonya? What's got into you?'

'Unlike your friend Margaret, nothing has got into me,' said your mum.

'What do you mean?'

Well, I can't repeat the rest of the conversation, Gene. Suffice to say it contained a lot of your mum's feelings about, how she put it, 'that floozy in Melbourne', then she hung up on me and now we only speak via the United Nations – which is how I describe your sister at the moment. We talk through Sharon.

I don't know what I can do. I wanted to talk to your mum about it when I got back and was going to own up and tell her what went on, which was nothing.

It's true Gene, I swear to you: nothing happened. I slept in one room and Margaret slept in another. You could ask anyone. Well, you could ask Margaret – I mean, she'd know, she was there.

The real point is nothing ever is going to happen because Margaret understands how your mum would feel about me having a sort of girlfriend affair, so we decided to just stay friends. We're too old to be having dramas over these sorts of things; you do that when you're 40, not at our age.

I don't know how it would have panned out anyway; I don't want to live with anyone again. Well, I live with Milton, but Milton's OK – he's a bloke, he's my mate and it's not the same thing. It's like sharing a shed, sharing a house with Milton.

Margaret made me wake up to myself I think. She said to me, 'You and Sonya had the big one Roly and you can't repeat it. You think you can sometimes, you never stop trying and that's the problem, you've got to stop. You can have something else, but you can never have what you had.'

I don't know what it is about the Jones family. They've all got an extra philosophical gene in them, because she's right. I can't see your mum and I ever living under the same roof again. On the other hand, if I'm honest, I can't see myself being hitched up with anyone else and that's what I wanted to tell your mother, the silly dill.

Anyway, don't tell your mother about what I've said here. I don't suppose it matters, does it? She'll find out soon anyway – bloody Beryl Coates will probably get hold of this letter from Mrs Phipps at the post office and steam it open.

Anyway Gene, I'd better scoot off. I'm having dinner with Sharon tonight and I've got to iron a shirt.

Give my regards to Ahmed and tell him I hope the ballet business is holding up for him. I hope you're both happy. Write soon.

Lots of love,
Your poor old dad

MILTON'S WEDDING NIGHT
POST-MORTEM

Kalangadoo, Monday

Dear Gene,

How are you son? Kicking with the wind still, are you?

By the way Gene, thanks for your letter. I see you've got the tape of Milton's wedding night, that's good.

I'm glad Ahmed liked the song. He's got very good taste, your ballet-dancing mate. What do you call him again? Your 'little Nijinsky' – is that Russian for ballet or something? By the way, how is Ahmed's ballet career going? Is he in anything at the moment? Keeping his feet off the ground is he?

Getting back to Milton's wedding – gee, it was a beaut turn, one of the best I've ever been to.

I tell you what, Athena's family, the Halicopolouses – there's a crowd who know how to have a good time. You know when you've been at a wedding with that mob – they hate a drink and a dance! Clarence Sims and the boys started playing 'Zorba' at about 11.30 and I don't think anyone sat down again for an hour and a half.

My bones were acting up something shocking the next day and my feet, they're just not used to it, Gene. I think I've got that Zorba's dance permanently etched in my brain.

The amazing thing is that the whole night there not one blue, not one fight and not one punch-up in the car park. Clarrie Sims and the band said they couldn't remember the last wedding they played at when there wasn't a scrap of some sort.

Even more remarkable considering the Wilson boys were there. Remember I told you Milton invited them? Gene, they were like angels – the Wilson boys! They actually got dressed up in suits. No one recognised them when they turned up at the church; I didn't, I'd never seen them in suits before. They'd even shaved, Gene! One or two people were saying they thought the Wilson boys had had a bath as well; they looked clean. People were actually sneaking around taking their photograph on the quiet, you know, as proof.

Well, you can imagine it Gene: if someone came up to you on the street and said, 'By the way, I saw the Wilson boys the other night at a wedding. They had suits on, they'd had a bath and a shave and behaved themselves all night', you'd turn around and say, 'You must have been shickered!'

Of course, it's all out of respect for Milton you see. I don't know the full story because Milton shies away from it when I bring up the subject, but when Cranky Frankie, their old man, died when the boys were just nippers, Milton must have helped their mother out financially, helped the family get back on their feet again.

He's always had a bit of a soft spot for the Wilson boys, Milton. I think he feels a bit sorry for them. I know he's tried to get them work over the years and he always sticks up for them and I forget how many times he's been in court as a character witness for one of them.

Anyway, I was a bit knackered for a few days after the wedding, Gene. We didn't get home until late, Margaret and I didn't get to bed until 5 am. Well, what I mean is, I would have dropped Margaret off at her house at about 4.45, so I must have got to bed at my place at around 5 am.

Anyway, Mr and Mrs Jones are off on their honeymoon to Phillip Island in Victoria, the place where all the little fairy penguins waddle out of the water at night. You sit around freezing your bits off for hours, wondering what possessed you, waiting for them to emerge before watching them shuffling into the burrows where they live. Sounds exciting. Well, interesting if not exciting.

Anyway Gene, I better get cracking. I'm packing up all my stuff and moving into my house next week so I've got a lot of fluffing around to do!

Give my regards to Ahmed and write soon.

Lots of love,
Your dad

BUSBY'S SALES SOAR

Kalangadoo, Monday

Dear Gene,

How are you son? You winning?

I'm all right myself, tacking to starboard with a southerly.

I am a bit euchred at the moment though. I spent half the week with Margaret in Mount Gambier buying stuff for my new house.

Talk about a man on a spending spree. I bought a fridge, a washing machine, an iron and ironing board, a lounge suite, a kitchen table and chair, I bought a bed lamp – just the one for me – and I bought a bed. I also bought $300 worth of kitchen gear and about half the world's supply of groceries.

So you can kiss your inheritance goodbye, Gene, I spent it all down at Busby's Electrical & Whitegoods Store down in Mount Gambier. I don't think the young bloke serving me at Busby's could believe his luck when I told him what I wanted. Boy, was he happy. 'This will surprise the boss when he gets back from lunch,' said the young bloke.

'Yeah,' I said, 'especially if my cheque bounces on you.'

'What do you mean?' asked the young bloke.

'Relax son, it's a joke,' I said. Irony-free zone that chap.

'Oh right, awesome!' he says, whatever that's supposed to mean, I don't know. But I tell you, I've never written out a cheque with that many noughts on it Gene.

Still, I had to buy all that stuff because when your mum and I parted the ways, I left everything with her – which is a polite way of saying your mum held onto everything for dear life. She's not stupid, your mother.

Living at Milton's I never needed anything in the way of furniture and things like that, but I nearly had a coronary when the young bloke added up the prices. I had to get Margaret to look over it and tell me what it came to. I'd tell you what it all cost Gene, but there are young people waiting to get married and I don't want to frighten them.

I was saying to Margaret I reckon when you split up a marriage, the party who is leaving ought to get a tax break to cover the cost of setting yourself up again with all the furniture and stuff. Either that or you ought to get a special discount at furniture and whitegoods shops. They ought to give you one of those plastic card things like a divorce card – that's what you could call it. Something that tells the shop that you recently separated and don't have a zac to your name. You could show a divorce card at these joints and they'd give you a discount. It's a good idea I reckon.

Anyway, shopping was exhausting enough, but I've had the painter and the plumber over at the house for the rest of the week. The painter has been painting what I asked him not to paint and the plumber has been running the plumbing through places I told him not to plumb in. It made a change from last week, which I spent fighting with the electrician.

I wanted some extra power points in the room and now I've got three more power points in a room that has already got three, that makes six. The two rooms that had only one power point and I wanted another put in don't have any now because he took the ones that were in there out.

I wanted a light put on the outside loo because it didn't have one and it still doesn't. The outside laundry has got one, in fact it now has two; he put one in there instead of the loo.

'What happened to the plan I drew up?' I asked this joker.

'I don't know mate, I never saw a plan.'

'I gave it to your boss.' I said.

'Wouldn't trust the boss with a plan,' he said.

'Why not?'

'Well, he can't read.'

'Are you saying he didn't give you the plan?'

'He gave me a bit of paper with something on it, come to think of it.'

'What was on it?' I asked.

'A plan of some description.'

I mean, what do you do with them Gene? Anyway, he reckons I'll have all the lights in before Christmas with a bit of luck, but I'm not taking my chances; he didn't tell me which year.

I better get a move on Gene. I've had a bit of chewy on my shoes today and I'm a bit behind. I'm spending my first night at the house tonight, on my own I hope. What

I mean is, on my own with the ghost they reckon lives down there, the ghost of old Mrs Mathieson.

I've got a plan to sort her out though. My snoring should be a very effective anti-poltergeist device.

Anyway, regards to Ahmed and write soon.

Lots of love,
Your dad

THE GHOST OF DOT MATHIESON

Kalangadoo, Monday

Dear Gene,

How are you son?

Bit better than me I hope. I'm not crook or anything, my nerves are just a bit shot. I haven't slept all week, that's the problem. It has been a shocker of a time over here, Gene.

You know I moved into my new house a week or so ago, don't you? Remember I was telling you how the railway line runs through the backyard and it splits into two? Well, Harry Rickman down at the real estate place absolutely assured me that no trains came through there at night.

But what woke me up at 1 am the first night I slept there, Gene, was the longest goods train I've ever heard. I thought at the time that it must be just a one-off. Next night, the same thing; at 1 am the goods train comes through, then the next night and the night after that.

By Friday night I was lying awake waiting for the bugger. I got up the next day and was so dark on Harry

Rickman that I rang him. I was tired Gene, I did my 'nana' a bit.

I said, 'Harry, you told me, categorically, there were no trains running past my place at night.'

'Yeah. That's right,' he said.

'You forgot to mention that there's a bloody goods train rattling past my joint every morning at 1 am!'

'What are you talking about Roly?' said Harry. 'There's no goods train.'

'Look Harry, I know you're a real estate agent so you can be a bit economical with the truth, but I don't like being completely lied to.'

'Roly, I swear, there's no goods train.'

'Harry, the longest goods train in the southern hemisphere rocks past my place at 1 am on the dot every night!'

'You're dreaming.'

'I am not bloody dreaming!'

'Roly, I'll ring the railways at Mount Gambier right now and check it out, you'll see.'

'Good, you do that Harry,' I said and hung up on him Gene. Hell, I was cranky.

Ten minutes later Harry rings back.

'What did I tell you Roly?' said Harry. 'I rang the railways, there's no goods train. There are no trains whatsoever after 4 pm in the afternoon! Perhaps you are having nightmares; are you on some sort of medication, Roly?'

'I am not having nightmares and I am *not* taking drugs,' I said.

So anyway Gene, by now I'm starting to think perhaps I *have* got a couple of kangaroos loose in the top paddock.

I rang Margaret, explained what was going on and asked her what she thought I should do.

'I'll need a witness,' I said.

Margaret said, 'Look dear, why don't I stay tonight? I'll bring my camera and when the train comes through I'll take a photograph, then we'll have proof.'

'That's a beaut idea, Margaret,' I said, hoping none of the town snoops were around to see her arrive at night and not leave until the following morning.

So around Margaret came – I slept in the spare room of course – and what happens? 1 am and no train Gene, I couldn't believe it! Now I'm thinking I'm going to get a visit from the blokes with the reverse white jackets any tick of the clock and they'll take me off to the funny farm.

I said, 'Margaret, you have to believe me, there *is* a goods train.'

'Yes dear, I am sure there is. Maybe it wasn't scheduled to run tonight,' said Margaret.

'Look, stay one more night.'

Margaret agreed to stay another night and, bugger me Gene, the same thing – no goods train.

'Yep, I'm losing my marbles, Margaret,' I said to her. 'Obviously I am no longer the full box of chockies.'

Anyway Gene, the upshot is the next night I am on my own and what happens? At 1 am the bloody goods train rattles through again! So I threw on my dressing gown, grabbed the torch and the camera Margaret had left and flew out the door and that's when it happened. The moment I flew out the door, the noise stopped. It was dead silent.

I shot down the backyard to the railway line and there was no train, Gene, no lights, nothing. I stuck my ear on the railway line to feel if there were any vibrations but still there was nothing. That's when I felt a big chill up my spine.

Then it got worse. The second I set foot back inside the house, the bloody goods train started up again. That was it, Gene. I ran outside, threw myself into the car and I was off like a bride's nightie, pyjamas and all, over to Margaret's. I've been there all week – only just got back a few hours ago.

You see Gene, I'm starting to believe they were right – here was no goods train – and that the house is haunted. It was old Dot Mathieson's ghost playing silly buggers with me.

I spoke to Milton and Athena about this and Athena has organised a Greek priest who did their wedding in Mount Gambier to come around with incense and try and smoke Dot out. Father Ryan offered to come over, wave around a thurible and try and coax her out as well.

Meanwhile, I spoke to your sister Sharon this morning and she reckons I should try communicating with old Dot, so that's what I've been doing. I've been wandering around the place trying to talk to Dot, telling her I love the house, that I want to stay and asking if she could ensure that if the goods train is going to go past, that it does so during the day. I feel like a dill and if old Dot is here, she's not saying much.

Anyway Gene, I'd better go. Regards to Ahmed and write soon.

Lots of love,
Your scaredy-cat dad

JACK SIMS & SANDY THE WALLOPER

Kalangadoo, Monday

Dear Gene,

How are you son? You winning?

I'm pretty good myself, haven't had a bad week at all.

What have I been up to? Not a lot – last night Milton
and I went down to the RSL Hall to farewell Sandy
Malloy. You know Sandy Malloy, the copper here in town;
he's chucked it in and retired. Had enough he reckons. I
don't know what the full story is, but I think he had a few
run-ins with the higher-ups in Mount Gambier, so Milton
was saying.

It was all over this Athol Pearce business – you remember
Athol Pearce, don't you? He used to go to school with you,
the one who called you a sissy and picked on you all the
time for playing skippy with the girls.

Well, Athol is one of those idiot, brain-dead local
councillors here in town. His wife, Stephanie, runs that
silly Committee Against Moral Decline; a bunch of
bloody wowsers the lot of them, running around the joint
telling people what's good for them. I never liked Athol

Pearce; never trust a man who reckons he's all good and no bad – he's lying through his teeth.

And talk about get up your nose about morals! They've even got a joke about it here in town: why is the Moral Decline Committee against sex? Because it encourages dancing.

Still, Athol Pearce must have had sex once because he's got a daughter, Felicity.

Anyway, what happened was a couple of months ago, young Felicity won the Citizen of the Year award, which came as no surprise to the grown-ups here. After all, her mum and dad were on the judging committee, so it was a lay-down misère. That's all right, but a couple of weeks ago Sandy Malloy nabs Felicity and a couple of her grammar school mates smoking drugs down by the creek near the railway station.

Don't know what it was, but think it was some of that marijuana stuff your sister had on her omelette in Bali. So Malloy catches them having a puff or whatever and instead of arresting the kids, he takes all their names down and goes around to see their parents and tells them he'll turn a blind eye to it this time, but if he catches them puffing on the green stuff again he'll charge them as quick as look at 'em – which is fair enough.

But then what happens is that one of the kids hits the panic button. He thinks he's going to get charged anyway, so gets onto his parents in Adelaide and they make a phone call to some higher-ups in the police department and the next minute, Sandy Malloy is being told by his boss in Mount Gambier that if he charges any of these kids, he might like to think about a career managing a police station on the Nullarbor Plain.

All of a sudden this whole episode has turned into something bigger than Ben Hur. To make matters worse, an idiot journalist from Mount Gambier gets hold of the story, from God knows where, and writes a stupid bloody article in the local newspaper saying that Kalangadoo is becoming the drug capital of Australia and demands to know what the local police are doing about it. The headline screamed, YOUNG DRUG DEALERS RUN RIFE IN KALANGADOO! Talk about a lot of bloody tripe, Gene.

As someone once said, 'There's only two things you can believe in an Australian newspaper: the price and the date.'

So of course, Athol Pearce and his stupid mob from the Committee Against Moral Decline start writing letters to the newspaper calling for the community to set up a local drug watch, a sort of Neighbourhood Watch for drug users. What a damn hypocrite – his daughter is one of them.

After this happened, Sandy Malloy decided he was jack of it all and retired from the police force early. He's going to go and live in Adelaide.

It's funny how things turn out for people, isn't it? Did I ever tell you about all that business with Sandy Malloy and old Jack Sims? You remember old Jack Sims? Of course you do, he was at your christening. Jack's dead now of course; he died about a year ago. You wouldn't find a nicer bloke than Jack Sims I reckon. The poor bugger had a drinking problem as we all know. It wasn't his fault; Jack got wounded during the war and came back with a crook leg and his nerves shot to pieces. Jack never drank before the war, but because of his gammy leg and the nerves, he looked like he was stonkered all the time.

Anyway, Jack was always getting picked up by the wallopers in Mount Gambier, even though he never drank. Eventually Jack decides if he's going to get thrown in jail for being a drunk all the time, he might as well become a drunk and enjoy himself, so that's what happened.

Jack was always a happy drunk and never caused any trouble; he'd just go wandering around the place laughing at the moon, not like some of those poor buggers who sit around outside the pubs down at the Mount yelling at people who go by.

At the time Jack first hit the turps, Sandy Malloy was a young copper in Mount Gambier and got to know Jack and learned what happened to him during the war. Malloy felt a bit sorry for him and would keep an eye on him to make sure the other coppers didn't rough him up.

So anyway, Sandy Malloy moves to Adelaide to work and as it turned out, so did Jack Sims.

Now, there was the murder in Adelaide one year and they put a photograph of the suspect in the papers, you see, and bugger me dead if the suspect isn't a dead ringer for poor old Jack Sims. So what happened was Jack was wandering around Adelaide and a couple of wallopers grab him and the next minute Jack is up on a murder charge.

Eventually Malloy gets wind of all this and knows Jack wouldn't tread on an ant, let alone kill someone, so Malloy checks out around the place to find out where Jack was at the time of the murder. It doesn't take him long to discover that Jack was in the drunk tank in Port Adelaide the day the murder was committed, so Malloy gets Jack Sims released.

He takes Jack home to his place to keep him out the way for a while, but then two days later, Jack goes down to

Alberton Oval to watch the Magpies play, has a few snorts and gets picked up again.

Well that does it for Malloy. He goes to the Adelaide lock-up, explains the situation to his boss and says to Jack, 'Look, we're going to keep you in the lock-up until we catch this bugger!' And that's what he did. Jack stayed there for two weeks until they found the suspect and arrested him. The coppers, knowing the full story, looked after Jack and even let him have a few drinks on the sly.

None of this story would have come out because Malloy never said a word to anyone about it, but then Jack Sims dies last year. It was sad; he fell asleep with a cigarette still alight and well, the chair caught fire and it was goodnight.

Anyway, when Jack's last will and testament is read out, it appears that while he might have been in the grip of the grape most of the time, he was sober enough to never forget what Sandy Malloy had done for him. Jack left Malloy everything he owned, including a five-bedroom house in Adelaide and about $20,000 in a savings account.

When the story got out and made the rounds of Kalangadoo and Mount Gambier, Malloy was very embarrassed. After all, it's a bit hard trying to pretend you're a tough cop when everyone in town knows you're really just a big bloody sook! So Sandy Malloy has called it quits and he's going to live in Jack Sims' house in Adelaide. Funny life sometimes, isn't it?

Anyway, I better get going. Give my regards to Ahmed and write soon.

Lots of love,
Your dad

MOIRA PENNINGTON &
THE ARTS FESTIVAL

Kalangadoo, Monday

Dear Gene,

How are you son? You winning?

I'm all right. I'm a bit exhausted, been flat out like a lizard drinking this past week. You know when you have those weeks when you can't get to the off switch?

We've had the annual Arts and Crafts Festival here during the last week or so, the one we have every year.

Anyway, because your mum and I have been on the radio a bit over the years, people around this way think we're sort of celebrities. I think it's a lot of hooey myself, but you know what it's like here Gene; you get famous around here if you get through on the talk-back line to the ABC in Mount Gambier.

So anyway, your mum and I got roped into opening a few things in the art exhibition, and I MCed the music turns. I've being enjoying myself too, but could do without the bloody politics around the place; there's been a few big blues going on down at the Shire Arts Council.

I was talking to Moira Pennington, Jack Pennington's wife. Jack's dead now of course, but you'd remember Moira the artist. She lives a couple of doors up from Fred Luscombe's widow, Ethel. Tall woman – she wore those bright bohemian-type dresses like your sister.

Anyway, Moira's been having a barney with a couple of the newer members of the Arts Council committee. Apparently a few of the Joan-come-latelys think there ought to be other things in the room where Moira's painting exhibition is hanging at the Crafts Centre.

They're saying there is a lot of wasted space on the floor and there should be some other sort of art put on the floor to fill the room up a bit. When Moira got wind of this she fronted up to one of the meetings and tore strips off them. She said to the other committee members that they could fill up the room with other things if they wanted to but it would be over her very dead body, or words to that effect. She's right too. I mean, as she said to me, 'You don't hang up serious paintings like mine alongside a macramé and quilting exhibition from the local sheltered workshop – it doesn't matter how bloody good the work is!'

Moira would know a thing or two about these things of course, because she had a painting hung out of town at a coffee lounge in Mount Gambier some years back during the sixties, she told me. So she's no slouch knowing how things are done in the artistic department.

There has been a huge carry-on about it all. They've had letters to the local paper from people saying it was yet another example of the tall poppy syndrome, and others saying Moira's work was interesting if you have a fascination for ghost gums and rural surrounds, but hardly a work of genius.

In the end, Moira threatened to spit the dummy and pull out of the festival, which resolved the argument quick smart because the council already had the invitations printed and there wasn't anyone else in town with enough paintings to mount a fill-in exhibition anyway.

Aside from this carry-on, we always have a literary event during the festival down at the bowling club on the Thursday night. People get up and read things they wrote or someone else's work. It was a beaut night and a good turn-out this year too, Gene. Your sister Sharon read from some book – what was it called again? Something about women who run with things, I forget exactly what it is they run with now – I think it was dogs or something… dingoes it might have been. I didn't understand much of it myself, but the women seemed to cotton on to it and Sharon read it really well.

Milton got up and read a few bits of his poetry he had lying around the place. Milton's stuff is more like poetic philosophy; it's all about life and understanding and how it affects your golf handicap. It went down really well.

Anyway, I better get a move on. The high school is putting on their first performance of Shakespeare tonight down at the Scout Hall and I've got to introduce the headmaster and welcome everyone along. I don't know how the play's turned out though; there have been a lot of problems with it apparently. A couple of the lead characters got caught shoplifting down at Mount Gambier during the week and the drama teacher had a bit of a nervous breakdown, so the science teacher had to step in to try to pull it all together. She was saying to me this morning down at the milk bar that if she couldn't find a replacement for Hamlet by 10 am they might have to call the whole thing off.

I better go, Gene, I've got to iron a shirt for tonight. Give my regards to Ahmed and say hello to his parents, will you? Write soon.

Lots of love,
Your dad

LAST ACT FROM MEDEA

Kalangadoo, Monday

Dear Gene,

How are you son? You winning?

I was, for a while. No doubt you've spoken to your mother by now, so I thought I might throw in my version of events for the history books.

Well, we had a blue as you know. It sort of ended all right, but it was awful there for a while. I knew it was about to happen Gene, I could feel it from three streets away on my way over to your mum's.

I could tell it was going to be bad because when I arrived the front door was already open. That wasn't a good sign; it meant your mother was positioning herself inside the living room waiting to attack. I walked in and she was standing next to the window, you know with the light coming in silhouetting her from behind. It gave her a sort of omnipresence.

Then it started.

'Of all the people I had to find out from, Roly – Beryl Coates, I had to hear it from *Beryl Coates*, didn't I?'

'Sorry Sonya, you weren't meant to,' I said looking at the ground.

'Sorry, I wasn't meant to find out from Beryl Coates, or sorry, I wasn't meant to find out full stop?' said your mother, the ice forming around the words as she spoke.

'Look Sonya—'

'Look? *Look?!* Where should Sonya look, Roly? Should Sonya look at the bus station where everyone who got off the bus over the last four days was informed by bloody Beryl Coates that my former husband of 50 years was about to enter marital bliss with some floozy who writes crime novels?'

'Sonya—'

'Shut up! I haven't finished. Maybe Sonya should look at the Women's Auxiliary meeting last night where every person in the room came up to me to say how sorry they were? As if a close family member had suddenly died. Roly, I know it was National Sorry Day yesterday, but I thought National Sorry Day was about stolen children, not ex-husbands,' said your mother.

'Sonya, please—' I protested.

'That lovely woman Jessie Milthorpe said sorry to me in the street yesterday, Roly.'

'Oh dear,' I said.

'Oh dear indeed, Roly. Do you understand the cruel irony of having an Aboriginal woman stopping you on the street on National Sorry Day and saying sorry to you, on the very night the Women's Auxiliary was saying sorry to Jessie? Do you have any idea what it was like for me?'

'Listen Sonya,' I said, 'if you're going to do the last act from *Medea*, will you cut to the last scene and get it over and done with?'

'Or maybe Sonya should look at her daughter Sharon or her son Gene, who have known about this forthcoming marital bliss for weeks and have been told by my former husband of 50 years that they should keep quiet. And why?'

'You know why,' I said.

'Why? Because you wanted to make sure *Beryl bloody Coates* found out before I did!'

'Sonya, that is ridiculous, you know that's not true. If I wanted Beryl bloody Coates to find out, I would have—'

'Done what you did,' interrupted your mother.

'I would have rung her and told her.'

'Well, you might as well have.'

'Look Sonya, you know as well as I do when it comes to gossip, Beryl Coates is bloody telepathetic!'

'Telepathic,' said your mother, correcting me.

'She's both!' I replied. 'Sonya, you told me yourself that Beryl had learned how to lip-read and understand sign language so she wouldn't miss out on any gossip.'

'How could you? How *could* you?' said your mother.

'What can I say?' I said. 'If I say sorry, you don't believe me. If I don't apologise, you say I'm a heartless bastard.'

'I'd say that you were both actually.'

'That would be right.'

'Well, why couldn't you just go and do it somewhere else?' said your mother.

'Do what?' I asked.

'Get married to Lana Turner somewhere else.'

'Listen,' I said, 'this is going to have to stop. Your referring to Margaret as Lana Turner or Rita Hayworth, or the bloody "shack-up" has got to stop. Her name is

Margaret Jones. If you want to talk about her, have the courtesy to call her by her proper name. I'm going,' I said, marching to the door. 'I'm really sorry you had to find out this way. I didn't mean it to happen that way, I was trying to avoid exactly this sort of confrontation. I should have just rung you up and said, "Hi Sonya, guess what? I'm getting married again – are you happy for me?" or maybe I should have just sent you a wedding invitation and let you find out that way.'

'Oh, stop it, you're going on like a two-bob watch,' your mum said as I turned to go. 'Actually, I don't give two hoots that you're getting married to Margaret whatever she's called. I knew you would – I wondered why it hadn't happened sooner.'

'What?'

'Well, I expected it. I'm not upset about her. If she can put up with your bloody snoring, good luck to her!'

'Well, what are you putting me through the Westing-house washer for?' I said.

'Beryl Coates!' said your mother. 'To think that she heard about it first and I didn't even have the drop on her. That's what I'm cranky about; you've humiliated me.'

'I didn't mean to,' I said.

'Am I getting an invite?' asked your mum.

'Are you serious?'

'Nup!'

'You can come if you want.'

'Well, if I do, I want to be the one who...oh, it doesn't matter.'

'What Sonya?'

'The one who tells Beryl Coates.'

It went on like that Gene. God knows with your mother, I don't understand it.

Anyway, I better go. I've got to go and pick Margaret up from the bus station and Beryl Coates is going to be on duty. I'm just working out how to mime the words to Margaret, 'When did the doctor say you were due?'

Love to Ahmed. Write soon.

Lots of love,
Your dad

HOLIDAY IN NOUMEA

Noumea, New Caledonia, Thursday

Dear Gene,

How are you son? You winning?

I'm doing all right. I'm over here in Noumea in New Caledonia at a holiday resort. Sharon and I got here a few days ago. Yes, you heard right: Sharon, your sister Sharon.

You wouldn't believe our rotten luck Gene. You know how Margaret and me were going on our first holiday together, well, five days before we were about to take off, Margaret comes down with a bloody inner-ear infection. Old Doc Wilson banned her from flying and swimming so she couldn't go. God, you don't have to be dead to be stiff, do you?

Anyway, I was going to cancel the whole kit and caboodle, but Margaret insisted that I still go and suggested I ask Sharon and see if she'd like to join me. To cut a long story short, that's what happened.

I know I've offended Peugeot the Car God – I cannot get the 404 to stay out of Snowy Thompson's garage, it's costing me a fortune – and now I've obviously offended Saint Christopher the patron saint of travellers!

I mean, a joker can't take a trick. I tell you, I wish I'd stayed at home, Gene. I don't know if you've ever been to one of these resort joints overseas with Ahmed, but it's not my cup of tea. It's terrific if you're young and single and looking for a new sparring partner to get hitched to, but at my age the last thing I want to do is sit around a swimming pool all day chatting up divorcees.

On top of that, there's the bloody noise Gene! They're on the go here day and night and there's nowhere peaceful to go. You're sitting there reading a book enjoying the quiet and the next minute some young French maniac appears from behind a bush somewhere with a microphone yelling, ''ullo everybody, it is showtime! My name eez Philippe and we're now going to av zee big surfboard race.'

It drives me bananas – I'm too old for it, Gene.

'C'mon! You join us, yes?' he says to me as I try to make a run for it.

'No thank you,' I'd say as politely as I could.

'C'mon, eet eez fun!' says the joker as 30 people around the pool start laughing at me.

'Look,' I said, 'I'm nearly 80. The ticker is not what it used to be and I don't intend to die in the middle of a swimming pool on the back of a surfboard, if you don't mind.'

Then he starts grabbing my arm. 'C'mon, you will love eet, c'mon!' says this lunatic.

I said to him quietly, 'Listen pal, what is zee French word for "go away or I'll hire someone to kill you"?'

Finally Sharon arrived and sorted him out. Since then I stay in the bar most of the day, which is not doing wonders for my liver. But it's like this from eight o'clock in the morning until eleven o'clock at night. It's a concentration camp where they kill you by making you have fun. I don't want to have fun; I want to have some peace and quiet.

And by the way Gene, do you think you can get a cricket score over here? No way! I mean we're getting done like a dinner over in India, and I've got to ring Margaret back in Australia to give me the score. I'd rather be in jail. At least in jail you could find out the cricket scores.

Oh-oh, sorry Gene, hang on a second. I've just spotted that woman from Sydney – the divorcee. Sharon reckons she's got her eye on me. I tried to put her off the other day when she strutted up to me. I said, 'Oh hello, how are you? Nice day? Yes, just finishing a letter off to my wife, she's in intensive care back home and couldn't come. Best keep at it.'

I had better find Sharon for protection. In fact I'd better go and protect Sharon; she's got half the male staff here trying to coax her into the bedroom.

So, I'll be off now Gene. Give my regards to Ahmed and write soon.

Lots of love,
Your dad

THE BIG SURPRISE

Kalangadoo, Monday

Dear Gene,

How are you son?

Well, Gene, what can I say? I couldn't believe your phone call last night, son! I was so excited I didn't know what to say to you. Here we are, not expecting you until Christmas and now we're going to see you this coming Sunday!

You and Ahmed living out here for three months while Ahmed is touring with the Royal Ballet is the best news I've ever had Gene. I tell you, you've made an old man a lot younger with that news.

Your mother is tickled pink too, of course. I got a phone call from battalion headquarters at 0800 hours this morning. The phone rang and I thought it would be your mother wanting to get operation Christmas Day underway. Sure enough, it was.

'You better get over this afternoon and we'll sort things out,' said your mum.

'What have we got to do?' I said.

'What? What have we got to do? Men, you are so stupid, I don't know why women bother with you,' said your mother.

'To help women move pianos,' I said.

'Yeah, well that would be the only reason.'

'You don't need to panic Sonya.'

'I am *not* panicking Roly, I am merely attempting to plan the comfort of our interstate and overseas guests. Someone's got to do it.'

'Sonya, will you move the cross on your back down-wind a bit? I'm getting smoke in my eyes.'

'What did you say?' said your mother.

'All right, all right, I'll come over at two.'

'One,' said your mother.

'One then.'

'No, make it 12.30, there's a lot to do.'

'All right Herr Capitaine, 12.30 it is.'

'Don't start that "Herr Capitaine" business with me, Roly Parks,' said your mother.

'Yes sir, no sir, three bags full sir.'

'Roly Parks, I'm warning you!'

So anyway Gene, that's where I've been all afternoon and I'm exhausted. I've got a list of things to do that goes from here to the Arctic Circle – should have them finished by Christmas.

And just when I thought the duties were finished, your mother hit me with a beauty.

'Now,' says your mother.

'Now what?'

'What about your fiancée, Rita Hayworth or Lana Turner or whatever her name is.'

'Her name is Margaret Jones, Sonya. What about her?'

'Is she spending Christmas Day with her brother Milton and his wife?'

'No, as a matter of fact, Milton and Athena are going up to Queensland to stay with friends over Christmas. I don't know what's going to happen; Margaret and I haven't talked about it.'

'Well, we'd better sort it out now,' said your mother. 'What are you going to do?'

'What do you mean? I've got my family here, what can I do? I can't be in two places at once, can I?'

'Well, you can't let the woman spend Christmas Day on her own either.'

'Well, what can I do?'

'You better invite her here,' said your mother, looking away.

'Invite her here? To what?' I asked.

'Christmas Day lunch, you idiot!'

'What, *here*? In this house? Christmas Day? You and Margaret in the same room?!'

'Well, she can't spend Christmas Day on her own, can she?'

'Where do you hide the sherry, Sonya? I need a drink.'

Well Gene, I couldn't believe my ears. You could have knocked me down with a feather.

'Are you sure about this Sonya?'

'No, I'm not sure at all,' said your mother, 'but I'd only be here feeling guilty that she was sitting around on her own on Christmas Day, so invite her.'

'What are you going to do to her? You're not going to slip her some Lysol are you?'

'I'm not going to poison her Roly! Look we may as well get it all over and done with, I'm obviously going to have to meet Lana at some stage.'

'Margaret.'

'Meet Margaret then, aren't I?' said your mum.

I was like a stunned mullet, Gene. I took a deep breath and said, 'All right, I'll invite her, that's very kind of you Sonya.'

'You don't have to go on about it,' said your mum, 'just invite her.'

'What about Wallace, are you going to invite him?'

'Wallace who?' said your mum.

'Your mate Wallace Whitfield.'

'Oh, that lounge lizard,' your mum snorted. 'I gave him the flick months ago.'

'I'm sorry to hear that.'

'I'm not,' said your mum. 'He was courting Beryl Coates behind my back.'

'Beryl Coates?! That's terrible Sonya, Beryl is such a good friend of yours.'

'I haven't spoken to either of them since. They deserve each other!' said your mother.

'I'm really sorry to hear that,' I said, desperately trying to suppress my laughter while lying through my teeth. 'I've just got to go to the loo Sonya, I'll be back in a second.'

There is a God after all, I thought as I sat on the can laughing my head off.

So there you go Gene, life's such a funny bloody thing, isn't it? Margaret's going to come and I'll need my heart pills on Christmas Day when those two meet. I thought I'd better warn you about it.

Anyway Gene, I had better go, I've got a lot to do. I won't write again, I'll see you at the bus station on Sunday at about two o'clock.

Lots of love,
Your dad

ACKNOWLEDGEMENTS

Roly and Sonya Parks from Kalangadoo were originally created by writer and performer Jody Seidel and myself in the mid-eighties. *Letter from Kalangadoo* was a later development from a number of earlier ABC radio series featuring the two characters.

Roly and Sonya Parks first appeared on radio on the community station 3RRR in Melbourne in 1987. Brief as that stay was for the 'couple', I wish to thank 3RRR for starting the journey that led to a national ABC radio audience.

Without the encouragement and collusion of the visionary Michael Ingamells at ABC Radio, many of my ideas during this period would never have received budget numbers. Michael gave me a creative freedom that is not visible at ABC Radio today. As an executive producer who understood the importance of allowing writers and performers a playing field, he is responsible for giving life on ABC Radio to *Roly & Sonya Parks*, *Sir Murray Rivers QC* and *Clarke & Dawe*.

Sue Howard, friend, outstanding broadcaster and former head of ABC Radio, initially commissioned the *Letter*. Sue gave me the confidence to find and use a radio form that would keep the two characters and Kalangadoo alive.

To all the program makers across ABC Radio in Australia who have willingly broadcast the various series from the beginning, in particular, producer Helen Richardson, I thank you all.

To Jenny Farthing, Maddy and Shelley for their eternal patience.

To Krista McClelland for the artwork and painstaking editing of stories written over a 26-year period, who didn't really pull her hair out in the process.

Finally, to Jody Seidel: without her original collaboration in creating *Roly & Sonya Parks*, the *Letter* would never have been written.